THINGS IN PLACE

also by Jerry Bumpus
Anaconda (a novel)

THINGS IN PLACE

by

Jerry Bumpus

FICTION COLLECTIVE NEW YORK

Acknowledgment for permission to reprint: to *Fiction International* for "Things in Place" (originally "Desert Matinee"); "Our Golf Balls": (c) 1974 by *Shenandoah*, reprinted from *Shenandoah: The Washington and Lee University Review* with the permission of the Editor; to *Descant* for "A Song of Old Fangles"; to *Epoch* for "Selling"; to *Transatlantic* for "The Idols of Afternoon"; to *The Colorado Quarterly* for "The Heart of Lovingkind"; to *The Iowa Review* for "Away in Night"; to *The Gar* for "Satisfaction"; to *The Falcon* for "Patsy O'day in The World"; to *The Seneca Review* for "A Lament to Wolves"; to *New Letters* for "Victims"; to *Lillabulero* for "In The Mood of Zebras."

This publication is in part made possible with support from the New York State Council on the Arts, and with the cooperation of Teachers and Writers Collaborative and Brooklyn College.

First Edition

Typesetting by New Hampshire Composition
Concord, New Hampshire
Library of Congress Catalog No. 75-10744
ISBN: 0-914590-14-6 (hardcover)
ISBN: 0-914590-15-4 (paperback)

Published by **FICTION COLLECTIVE**

Distributed by George Braziller, Inc.
One Park Avenue
New York, New York 10016

for Bettie, Margot, and Prudence

CONTENTS

THINGS IN PLACE

The dust cloud followed the arroyo down to the valley and turned when it reached the highway, as Haskel knew it would, fanning wide on both sides of the road and coming straight toward him.

Haskel pulled the truck off the road, cut the motor, and rolling down the window leaned out. He heard far off a buzzing roar like a storm of hornets. He took out his teeth and put them in the breast pocket of his denim jacket. Then rolled up the window and drove on slowly, half-off the road to give them plenty of room.

Still over a mile away he could make them out, thirty or forty abreast so they wouldn't get their own dust. At this distance they were giant insects.

For three days and nights they had been out here, and Haskel had watched them. (Now for the first time they saw him—the flanks of the wide line drew in and they came even faster.) He had watched with binoculars and concluded that above all they were constantly in motion, even at night in their camp, jumping on their motorcycles and riding off as if they all had been stung by the same dire impulse. Or they danced all night, and he saw fights in the yellow light, and they rode around and around the bonfire, though in the distance it appeared they rode into the bonfire and became the fire itself—out of existence on a dare and back again. In the light of day they plunged headlong, whether down the highway, along a trail, or straight across the desert—they didn't need roads. They shot off hills, cutting through the air forward-leaning and furious, as if enraged with the passivity of space.

Five hundred feet ahead of Haskel they slowed. Now they would block the road.

There were even more than he thought—fifty, sixty. Women rode double behind some of them, lean long-legged women in jeans and leather, their faces shrewd as chromium, their eyes rapacious but at the same time paradoxically indifferent—as though their minds were elsewhere, or *they* were in fact elsewhere and these were their souls, fled to the desert. The men were big, long-armed, etched with tattoos. Grinning, their mouths were slashed with the obscene eagerness of wolves. Astraddle their bikes, revving the motors, they tightened a gantlet down the middle of the road, and as Haskel entered they leaned on the truck and pounded the fenders, grinning in at him.

Then he was through them. In the mirror watched them spread out again in a line. When they were at least two miles down the road Haskel put his teeth back in.

He slowed at the arroyo road. Up there was their camp. After glancing in the mirror, Haskel drove by. If he went up there, they might see his dust and come back.

He went down the highway to the dirt road that led to his place. And nothing beyond but the canyon rim and, over it, the first of two buttes staring at each other across forty miles. He called them the Big Ideas. Because they looked sure of why they were here.

The truck bounced, tilted on the road, slowly climbing the canyon wall. Then he saw the cabin. A window, crooked chimney, a shed out back. Beyond a narrow meadow, cut with a stream, a forest spread to the rim.

Haskel got out and held his breath, listening. Heard in the woods the crash of hard running. Then the dog, gray-brown, quick and wolflike except it didn't have the absolute, improbable bigness of a wolf, came out of the woods and into the meadow. Haskel squared off to meet it and it lunged against him and banged its jaws in his face, just short of his nose. He choked it, it chewed his shoulder, they stagger-waltzed a big circle and crashed against the truck. Haskel sat on the running board, panting, and the dog stood in front of him, panting too, tongue out, eyes laughing. "The motorcycle people," Haskel announced. The dog shut its mouth, ears pricked. "All of them. We had a parley-vous."

Haskel unloaded the supplies from the cab of the truck and went to the shed to chop wood. The dog wandered off but came back when it saw Haskel walking from the stream toward the cabin with the bucket. They went in and ate.

Later they went out front, watched the valley go down in purple. The sky became night. Abruptly the lights of Lordsburg thirty miles away winked into being.

In the middle of the night the cabin moved. He sat up. The dog, sleeping on the floor beside the bed, stood and yawned in the dark. Haskel went to the door.

Wind—huge and preoccupied, moved down the canyon, shaking loose, changing.

Haskel got the binoculars, moved them slowly up the arroyo, looking for the yellow light of the bonfire.

"They're gone," he said. The dog wagged its tail.

He built a fire and put on coffee. The dog curled down and went to sleep.

When the coffee was ready Haskel cooked breakfast. "They're gone for good," he whispered. He ate some and put the rest down for the dog when it woke.

Motor and headlights off, down the long hill the truck rolled, silent except for the creaking of springs and the skee of brakes. Haskel stopped short of the highway, staring at the dim corona above Lordsburg. He turned on the radio and found what he liked—cat music, he called it, coarse and jangling, from Mexico and fading off in miles, laced with static, then coming back louder than before.

An immense breath, change moved over the valley. First light.

He switched off the radio, started the motor, and pulled onto the highway.

He reached the arroyo road as gray dawn opened the sky. The hills were purple-black.

He walked around the bowl where they had camped. The wind

had scavenged footprints and tire tracks, and everything else it could take. Left behind a ripped-out beercase wedged between two bushes. And some cans scattered here and there, half-buried. Haskel kicked through the remains of the bonfire—the charred carcass of some huge beast they had cooked whole and ate on the ground. He moved farther out, circled the camp. Snagged in a bush he found a silk scarf, black and green. He sniffed it but already the desert had taken the smell of the person.

Instead of returning down the arroyo he drove out a trail they had cut with their motorcycles. It forked then crossed other trails. He turned onto one. And it crossed other trails. These were their streets, a city with no houses or people. He swung a turn, topping a dune, the nose of the truck in the sky, and when it dipped Haskel slammed on the brakes.

Two of them sat in the middle of the trail leaning against each other, a big one and a little one. Long hair, and wore pants but not shirts. Their backs were gray. Maybe the big one was dead, the little one propping him up.

They turned. The big one had a huge sharp chin, making him devilish, self-sure. He stared at Haskel, seemed to already start telling him what to do. The little one got up and helped him to his feet—and the little one was a woman, a girl, her hair hiding her face and partially covering her breasts. The man put his arm over her shoulders, leaned on her, and they came around to the side of the truck. Haskel rolled down his window.

She pushed her hair back with one hand. Her face was small and round. After looking at each other for a moment, she and Haskel spoke at the same time: "What are you doing out here?"—and she said, "Take us."

"To Lordsburg?" he said.

The man lifted his head, his eyes bright black. "No."

"No," the girl said to Haskel, her lips straight, smug.

"We got to stay awake," the man said and swayed back on his heels.

"Away," the girl said, grabbing him with both arms. "Away."

"You're staying out here?" Haskel said.

The girl stepped up on the running board. Leaning in, her face nearly touching Haskel's, she whispered, her eyes gleaming with excitement: "Take Hopalong and me to your place."

"My place?" He nodded. "Okay. Get in."

She went around the truck with Hopalong and opened the door. She stood behind him and pushed to get him up into the truck—and before he was even inside, sprawled knees wide apart, Haskel smelled blood and saw Hopalong's pants were soaked. The girl jumped in after him and slammed the door. "I'm Lily."

Haskel nodded and started the truck. Hopalong's head thunked against the rear window. Lily stared across him at Haskel, her face gray and without expression, her eyes like paraffin.

They helped Hopalong into the cabin and he shoved them away. He sat down at the table and grabbed up the cards with which Haskel played solitaire. His big fingers fumbled with the piece of string tied around the deck, then he shuffled the cards. Grinning fiercely, his bulging cheeks knotting his eyes, he rapped the cards on the table. "Stud," he said slyly and winked at Haskel.

"Come on," Lily said, tugging at his arm. She took the cards from him and pulled harder—"Over here. Come on, Hopalong." He got up and when he looked away from Haskel his mouth fell open, as if discovering the cabin was vast, infinite, with long corridors of light: far away, tiny in the distance, he saw a bed.

He collapsed across it. Haskel was building a fire when he heard a splop and turned to see the bloody trousers in the middle of the floor. With a piece of kindling he carried them out to the shed. When he returned, Hopalong, covered with blankets, lay turned to the wall. Lily wore one of Haskel's shirts, the sleeves rolled up. She was frying bacon and when it was done she took it to Hopalong and whispered too low for Haskel to hear.

"Hopalong won't eat." Haskel looked up. She stood beside him, her hands on her hips. "He used to eat all the time—you know? He was almost famous, he ate so much. Now, nothing. What'll I do?"

Haskel nodded. "You came to the right man: I don't know."

He went outside. The wind was up, rushing down the canyon like a big reckless boy. Haskel ducked around the corner. The sky scooped deep into the valley, a storm moving in. There would be snow, a great wall of snow.

The dog sailed around the corner on a gust of wind. "She kick you out?" Haskel yelled and grabbed its tail. The dog snarled, jerked its head around and snapped at him. When he let go it lunged away and barked. Haskel barked back, and the dog liked that, its eyes gleeful.

The food she cooked for Hopalong was on the table. Haskel sat down and ate it.

Then he built up the fire and got his pipe. He pulled up his chair and almost immediately was lost in the flames' invention. He returned only when, floating up from canyons, he put on another log.

The dog lifted its head, ears pricked. Slowly Haskel turned.

Lily wore only the shirt now, the shirt tail reacing halfway down her thighs. She tiptoed across the room and leaned down to him. Then her face went blank, her eyes faded as if she had forgotten everything.

Hopalong is dead, Haskel thought. That was it. He didn't need to ask her.

"I'll sleep here," Lily whispered.

He heard her making a pallet on the floor behind him. Then she was still, there was nothing but the fire and the wind above the cabin. When he woke, the fire was down and the wind had lain. The sky had the dense silence of snow.

He looked over his shoulder; she lay in a ball under the blankets, her head covered. On the edge of the pallet the dog also lay in a ball, its eyes open, staring at Haskel.

Morning. Haskel went out into a gray lull. A great drift buried half the cabin. Below, through thick air, the valley was shallowed with snow and seemed so close Haskel could have climbed to his roof and jumped clear across it. The woods had moved nearer during the storm, the trees immense and dour, shadows deep as caves hunkering under the branches sagging with the weight of the snow.

Haskel tromped out to the shed and got the ax, logs. Scooped off the block and a place to stand, and swung the ax. The log split with a sharp crack that shot down the hill, and Haskel looked up. Air quivered around the cabin. The door slowly opened.

Roaring, Hopalong ran out naked into the snow, his back and shoulders brownish yellow, waxen. The roar hung in the air. He ran hard, then stopped, bent forward, coughing.

Haskel ran down to the cabin, then onto Hopalong's trail. He caught up just short of the woods. "Hold it." Haskel panted. Louder—"Hold it!"

Hopalong swung around, reared, rising and opening his arms like a bear turning on dogs, and Haskel saw the huge wide chest, the stomach black with hair wedging down to the bush at the base of the stomach, as if pointing to what Haskel didn't see. For there was not the big thrusting cock Haskel expected. Instead, a gash grinned blood over a white sprig of tendon. Running pumped fresh blood over what had dried on Hopalong's thighs, ringing the snow red around his knees.

Haskel looked up to the man's face and could tell by Hopalong's eyes that he didn't know if Haskel had seen or not, that Hopalong no longer *knew.* Had somehow forgotten what there was about him that another man would find amazing. Hopalong's eyes, large and baffled, hardly paused on Haskel, as if Haskel were just one of a crowd floating before him in the gray light.

"Let's go back," Haskel said.

"Huh?"—and his eyes found Haskel.

"Back to my place. Come on."

Slowly shaking his head, Hopalong made the noise again, the roar that was almost a word but just outside meaning, louder and louder, and he clenched his fists and drew them up. Haskel backed but not fast enough, Hopalong was on him like a falling tree.

Numb deep in snow. Not thinking now. For minutes, maybe longer. Haskel was far away from himself, though now he saw his hands, red with cold. His hands were pushing at the yellow sack of flesh that was the naked man, and with strange easiness Haskel pushed him away.

Haskel sat up, breathing hard and looked at the sky. His face was blunt numb, maybe he no longer had a face, accepted the possibility that he didn't: Hopalong had lost his cock and was going around taking faces.

Thirty feet away Hopalong and Lily sat side by side in the snow, their backs to Haskel. They were talking low but in the silence Haskel heard them distinctly. "To Phoenix," she said.

"No. Nothing," Hopalong said.

"Bubba's there. And Nadine."

"Is that Bubba?" Hopalong said and looked over his shoulder at Haskel.

"No," Lily said. "That's just *him.* We can sleep in his house."

Hopalong got to his feet and moved away slowly, Lily calling to him. Haskel rose and started after him, running easily, the snow carrying him on waves.

Hopalong entered the first line of trees and disappeared. Then Haskel saw him again, slipping in and out of view, gliding deeper into the woods. Haskel followed, running hard, but looking over his shoulder he saw the cabin below, a straight line of woodsmoke rising from the chimney.

Ahead, Haskel saw Hopalong down a straight corridor through the woods. Going downhill now, they flew through luminous blue-green silence.

It would be a matter of minutes, an hour or two at most. The fire crackled excitedly, the flames danced.

"We can go to Albuquerque," Lily whispered. Hopalong lay flat on his back. Lily leaned down, her hands on his chest, her lips to his ear. Hopalong's eyes were closed and he breathed heavily, his lips flubbering.

Then he was silent. Lily stopped whispering. Haskel turned. She sat on the side of the bed, her legs crossed and her hands in her lap, watching Haskel with the corners of her mouth tucked up primly.

They dragged Hopalong out to the truck; nothing could get him there. Hopalong sat stiffly at the steering wheel, ready to go. Haskel slammed the truck door and he and Lily went into the cabin.

Lily sat at the table and picked up the deck of cards and shuffled them. Haskel rolled her a cigarette and one for himself. "Thanks," she said and dealt.

"My mom says, 'Lily, someday you'll get into something you can't get out of.' I tell her, 'Moms, don't lose any sleep worrying about me.' But maybe she's right.

"Some people just don't care–you know? Bubba don't care. He don't give a shit for anything. When Nadine got busted in Cruces she called Bubba and Bubba said, 'Tough shit.'" She was silent as they played the hand. She won.

She took the papers and tobacco and rolled another cigarette. Then she shuffled and dealt again.

"Mom says, 'Lily, you're crazy.' She says that because of what happened to Frieda. Frieda's my sister. Not my little sister, her name's Nadine. But Frieda's my big sister that got killed in a crash on Looper Lane in Phoenix. And Mom won't let me forget, like it was my fault. So I tell her if I'm crazy it's because she drove me crazy talking about Frieda. That's what Bubba tells me. Me and Bubba were doing Cunt City when I met Hopalong."

She ground out her cigarette and stood. She pulled the shirt up and over her head as if it were a sweater. With both hands she smoothed back her long hair, her breasts rising and slowly lowering. She came around the table and stepped between Haskel's knees. Putting an arm around his neck, she cupped a breast and put the nipple to his lips. "When Frieda got it she was riding back of Bubba. Bubba swerved to miss a Jag and went up the back of a Mercury and jumped a Pontiac Le Mans and a Chevvy van before they came down. Frieda never knew what hit her, but she died with a smile on her face."

Lily took off her trousers and lay naked on the bed. She crossed her legs, resting her ankle on the raised knee of her other leg. "Frankly, I can take it or leave it. Not like Nadine, who has to have it at least every ten hours and if she don't she gets nauseous. But Frieda was just the opposite. Doing it gave her gas, so she quit. She hadn't done it for six days when she racked up on Looper Lane.

"You got a nice one. You should've seen Hopalong's. It really was what you'd call remarkable. That was why the Motor Maniacs cut it off. Bunch of jealous little pricks—that's what I told Hopalong. But it didn't console him enough."

As Haskel lay down, Lily jumped up. She ran across the room, turned, her arms spread wide against the wall behind her. "Ready?" She squatted like a frog, her knees wide apart, and leaped. She sailed through the air and landed on Haskel.

Her hair hung down, framing their faces. She smiled brightly. "There! Gottum Daddy's whanger."

Lily got out, slammed the door, and stood beside the road. Haskel scooted down, it would be a long wait.

But then he heard on the silence a flat gray hum. He looked. A dot wavered on the horizon. Then gradually louder, the sound of a motor, tires on concrete. The dot became a car, its windshield glinting. It came fast though by now the driver could see Lily beside the road, thumb out, her other hand on her hip.

The motor cut, there was the strain of brakes and tires, and the car stopped beside Lily. The man at the wheel sat looking straight ahead as Lily got in. The car accelerated, and Lily looked out, but not at Haskel. Her face behind the window disappeared as the car smoothly sped off, two, three miles away, shrinking to a gray speck.

Haskel drove the truck onto the highway and headed the opposite direction, toward Lordsburg.

He hadn't gone far when a caravan of cars pulling horse trailers passed him. When he came to town more cars and trailers were parked along the street.

He parked the truck on a side street. When he walked back, on the main street twenty or thirty women wearing white ten-gallon hats and white leather jackets and pants with long fringe, were riding palominos. The women smiled and waved at the people. They rode two blocks down the street, turned, and rode back.

Haskel bought supplies, then headed back out, driving slowly down the straight highway, looking off across the plain widening with afternoon shadows.

He and the dog went to the shed to see how Hopalong was doing. He sat waiting in the corner. In a day or two when the snow was off Haskel would put him in the meadow.

Haskel went into the house and ate supper. He sat at the table a while, then moved across to the bed and was asleep before sundown.

He woke to the wind, or maybe it was a coyote. But again he heard the dull snow-muffled clomp. He went to the window.

They came single file, a long procession, more than he had seen in town, all in white leather with fringe and big white hats, all riding palominos shining in the night.

He backed away and stood in the middle of the room with his hands lifted. Then turned, grabbed up a log and threw it on the fire. As he heard the shudder-snort of the horses just outside the door he reached for the coffee pot. He had just banged it on the grate when the door opened wide and he turned to see the first of them leaning forward to clear the doorway as she rode into the cabin. The horse's eyes were huge, dazzled by the light.

OUR GOLF BALLS

Imagine the spray of atoms jolted out of the golf ball's very being by the impact of the driver. In a close-up we see the ball's upper-half spilling over the sharp edge of the club, while the lower-half begins the incredible flight.

You believe the golf ball achieves maximum velocity at impact, but in fact this occurs several yards from the tee, and at the moment of greatest speed, when at its finest as a golf ball, it is flat, squashed against the air, an odd oblong resembling in my excellent photographs a forward-leaning ghost stumbling through space.

Exactly how fast is our golf ball traveling? We all would of course like to know, but even our most careful estimates smack of the wayward melancholy of oafs speculating in a pasture: Is there a face in the sun? Is a beautiful thing always beautiful or does it give over? In Heaven where will we pee—in the clouds? Science has turned its back on the question of the golf ball's speed, thick-headedly assuming accelerologists settled the matter in the days of the immortal Tommy Armour! But a safe and considered estimate of the golf ball's maximum velocity is 450 miles per hour.

Carefully following its flight, we find it not only stumbles, it goes end over end: a ludicrous, not to say dizzying, moment unequaled in human experience—as far as we live to tell. During this moment the golf ball would, if it could, lose consciousness. I have paused to watch men and women in similar moments of excruciation;I'm sure you've watched too; we shall be watched when our time comes. Our shrinks slyly assure us we blot out the ultimately insufferable, but there are those who seem unfazed during great moments: our true heroes! They are capable of grandeur because they remain miraculously inviolate through those occasions when Heaven and Hell are one, when all things swirl off into light, and great Nothing roars like the sea. But they are shamming. They are no braver than our golf ball silently squealing its terror through space, and I have proof—a photo in which a racer is blurrily seen at the moment he sets a speed record: he hunkers in the cockpit of his jet-powered, 50,000-pound, 4-wheeled bullet, his face invisible beneath the black visor of his helmet. In this priceless photograph we penetrate distance, the blur of speed, the black visor, and see that our hero's moment of ultimate triumph is also his moment of ultimate shame: he's driving 900 miles per hour with his eyes shut!

We left our golf ball going through space end over end. Sun—earth—sun . . . Then the silent descent, the deep breath of sanity.

The ball lands, hops along, stops, and can be seen, an object no bigger than the end of my thumb, from a distance of 300 yards. How can this be?

After a tee shot the ball quite easily, though miraculously, sprawls! It is one of those ominous, necessarily shunned but daily miracles which crowd our days, making us yearn for boredom.

It's again itself—a tidy, round golf ball—when the player, clutching a club with a shiny steel head, comes tromping up. The player glances about, as if to see if anyone is watching, then drawing back, he begins viciously hacking the ball. The golf ball becomes an intimate of the two-iron, the three-, the inexorable five-iron.

The golf ball lies on the green which is a sloping sky. Little taps send it rolling up and down—but in the wrong direction! It is being aimed toward a hole in the sky, and each time it passes it hears the cold suck of wind down the hole. Other balls slide up and down, and our golf ball looks off, as only golf balls can, as one by one the others slip their grip and are gone.

We stand atop tall buildings and look at the cars and tiny people below. 100 stories is as high as we dare go; higher, and we lose interest in looking down and, staring off, expect planes, birds and soon, vaguely, even things of miraculous bearing. We also stand, the tribe of Man, at great cracks and look at the rivers writhing below. But always we stand firmly on the earth. We may throb with the bigness and looseness of things—"Ah! A wide vista!"—and we may suffer somewhat. But the earth is under our feet and we can always see the bottom of things.

Our golf ball, though, slides down a green sky that slants to a hole, and there's no wide vista: imagine looking into a hole, lit by tiny pinpoint light bulbs, four inches wide and a mile deep.

If you have succeeded in this, next imagine you are a golf ball. (Densely round. Squint. Clench your teeth.) Ready?

Fall.

A golf ball loves a golf course without holes. Such courses exist, though golf as we know it is not played there.

One such course exists as vividly for me as it did in my student days when I played there between classes and on weekends, and I can see it even more distinctly than I could then, for the course was in a brick courtyard between the west stands of Stagg Field and an adjoining building, and the sky above, during my stay in Chicago, was dark and heavy with snow. Beyond was the football field where people ran up and down yelling. But on the strip behind the stands there was only our fraternity of special golfers. The course was roughly 40 feet long by 20 wide; the walls rose 100 feet. High in one wall was a window covered with a heavy screen in which many golf balls were stuck.

This area was a proper size for chip-shots though there was no grass. I also took pleasure in raw Knock-O: I would wind up with my driver, hit the hall with all I had, and duck! The ball ricocheted and the walls groaned in profound vibration. One Sunday morning six or seven of us were down there, all teeing off at the same time, when a man in a smock opened the window. He called down that we were disturbing him and his colleagues. We agreed to leave if he would free the balls stuck in the screen. He disappeared and in a moment returned with a little silver hammer with which he knocked the balls out. We caught them on the fly. Years later I recognized the fellow in photographs: he was none other than Enrico Fermi!

We should consider driving across creeks, ponds, lakes. But we go next directly to where all golf balls end. On the bottom of the little round lake that lies between every number seven tee and every number seven green, there's a veritable throng of golf balls, but they lie in isolation: the murk of the lake and the bleakness that inks their vision (had they eyes) from seeing their hand before their face (had they hands, faces) makes each wholly alone.

They lie there forever. Or it seems forever to them. But you and I know that boys and sometimes big golf-ball-slugging men sneak out nights and, taking off their clothes, wade out to scavenge lost golf balls.

It is simple, it is fun.

He parks his wife's station wagon on the gravel parking lot and tiptoes down the fairway, gray under the moon. It is 2:30 a.m.; the clubhouse closed at midnight. Our golf ball poacher glances over his shoulder at a black line of trees under which he believes he sees movement—not the blur of a single person, but, impossibly, the surge of a gang—midnight loonies, experimental murderers! His heart pounding loudly, he stands frozen, hoping they can't see him. He strains to become invisible . . .

But he would be plainly visible clear to the clubhouse.

In fact, let's go up to the clubhouse, dark and silent, smelling of cigarette smoke and booze. Look out the window across the pellucid fairway bordered with trees on the right, a creek down the left. That's him, there, at 150 yards rather resembling a strayed shrub. Now he's moving on; bright fellow, he realized it wasn't a gang he saw, only shadows.

Before we go, I want to show you a picture.

On a long wall in the bar are at least a hundred photographs of professional golfers, politicians, movie actors, past club officers, and sundry local potentates whose identities have slipped, though they continue smiling. Those readily recognizable, the famous, were in all cases passing through en route to Chicago; they would stop long enough to hit a golf ball off that very tee outside our window, drink a gin rickey with the fellows, and have their picture taken. The photo in the corner is one of a kind, a true buried treasure: for over thirty years, incredibly, the bartenders, the club pros, the clubhouse presidents and their underlings, have had absolutely no awareness of the photo's rarity. Come here.

In the moonlight we see it clearly, not a large picture, five men standing shoulder to shoulder. They wear knickers, soft caps, sweaters, and the sloping background is the same fairway we see by turning slightly.

In the center is the immortal Tommy Armour! Because he is in this group, the picture will hang in the bar for as long as this clubhouse shall stand. The bar and the clubhouse are immortalized by this picture and the rather square-faced man in it. As for the rest, they are left to right: Russell Quinn, club pro; Henry Herring, club treasurer; Armour; Clarence "Fuzzy" Wooten, local banker and corn nabob; and Enrico Fermi!

Passing through en route to Chicago, Fermi stopped to hit a golf ball. He said hello to Tommy Armour, who also just happened to be passing through, and went into the bar with Armour and the others, had a gin rickey, then came out and stood . . . there.

He isn't smiling at the camera. "Fuzzy" Wooten appears to be laughing. At his own joke, likely. Armour is dour but alert; perhaps he is thinking of hitting another golf ball, or having another gin rickey. But Fermi is expressionless. *He* isn't thinking of golf balls or another drink. He must get on to Chicago . . . .

Our golf ball poacher has reached the lake and discovered it has shrunk. He whines softly.

Far enough at the back of his mind so he doesn't have to admit it, our poacher believes the world runs on magic. All day he's aware of the placid jury of clocks looking on, he feels the homage of desks and swivel chairs, and with acquaintances all day he gets and gives, and has careful conversations with strangers. Things usually stay put and when there's a slip he looks the other way. But nights in bed he closes his eyes and gives over—it all must end and begin again! Grinning, he skids down the long cloud hill and attacks the camps of friend and foe alike, ripping and tearing. Instantly the rampage widens, across the land people stagger forth in pajamas. The sky is burning, and all the streets and rooms and people, so laboriously put together, come undone. Every meaning and scrap of sense is scattered in trembling hunks. Poor fellow! Till dawn he tries to find his way home, stumbling through such debris it's as if the soup of the universe had sloshed out some of its logic for him to study. But wait! All is not lost. A bespectacled baboon in starred wizard robes and pointy hat, is sifting through it. Tries to fit this to that—Hipbone connected to the . . . telephone. Tosses the parts over its shoulder and, peering over the rims of its glasses, titters self-consciously. Can the baboon get the job done by morning? Indeed it does—and that, our poacher fellow is convinced, is the magical marvel of regeneration! For things work just as well as the day before—clocks tick tidily on, swivels swivel as sweetly as ever, and people will people with him again.

So when he sees the lake, black under the moon, is shrunken, he for a slow, dismaying moment believes the magic has started at its usual time—and during that long moment it's a hard balance for him.

But it passes—he goes down the hill and in the high grass at the edge peels off his sweatshirt, kicks off his shoes and takes off his socks and then his trousers.

Clutching his telescoping ball-retriever in one hand and a pillowcase in the other, he grits his teeth and wades through the ankle-deep mud. He stops. He had no idea the lake was so muddy: he had pictured the golf balls in rows on a lake bottom as smooth as the blue concrete of the club swimming pool, and he had even seen himself, in goggles and snorkel (and once even in scuba gear) agilely upside-down plucking balls from the lake bottom.

He is sinking in the mud. He pushes on toward the water—and suddenly sinks clear to his knees. But it's only mud. He lurches on, and is at last in the water, splashing so loudly he's certain he can be heard up at the clubhouse, and the mud is even deeper than at the edge—he is sinking smoothly. But struggling farther out, he gains buoyancy.

All right, he whispers.

He feels along the bottom with his feet. But he can't tell when his feet are in the watery mud and when they're lifted out. And while feeling around with one foot, the other subtly sinks. He moves farther out.

As in his better fantasies,under the moon the lake is speckled with celestial golf balls. He'll dive for them!

First, get the face and head wet. He bobs. There. Not so bad, was it? Yes. The water smells yellow. He keeps his tongue inside the good cage of his teeth.

Under again. Lean out and stroke powerfully with both arms—let go the retriever; the cork handle will float it . . . .

He leans out.

He is under water.

From the high west bank we watch the ripples precisely radiating from the center of the lake. The final ring commemorates his head. Then a turbulence churns the water. That was his stroke pulling him down for his glide along the bottom!

He can't open his eyes. Fiercely holding his breath, he is suspended horizontally beneath the surface—hovering as in his imagination, but not deep enough. And he cannot make himself go deeper!

He realizes that he is a great fool.

He is not out of air, but he heads for the surface, stroking powerfully toward air . . . .

He shoots waist-high from the water and when he sinks back he goes completely under!

There's no bottom! He's farther out than where he dived, and there's a drop in this lake, as there is in every lake and pond in our land. These drop-offs remind the unwary that small things hide whole mysteries. The drop-off is crude, but it has the quality; we're reminded of endless lines, special yearnings, tilted hills, knobless doors, immense cheeses, sudden circles, swastikas in a row, blue stones, giant mushrooms.

He thrashes. Swims wildly. Tries touching bottom—and goes under again!

He earnestly strokes to the surface (he has let go the pillowcase), and gulps air.

His imagination snaps a side view of himself treading water beyond the drop-off, the lake bottom far below.

He swims. Now put the feet down . . . . No. Not yet. They might again touch nothing. He swims farther toward the black shore . . . .

Now?

He lowers his feet—and his knees then his hips then elbow and right arm sink in mud!

He yells. It carries across the fairways and in the distance sounds like someone calling *Fore*.

He flops onto his back and pulling the arm free, strokes hard. He floats—the water here isn't deep enough for him to swim. He floats—the water here isn't deep enough for him to swim. He floats and his feet drag, and unavoidably he imagines the two furrows his heels trace in the mud, and he knows that if he tries now to get to his feet he will drown in mud.

Staring straight into the sky, he believes he is turning from the shallows. Good. He must float to deeper water, then slowly lower his legs, one at a time, and touch down . . . .

But he can't see the lake bank. Where is the deep water?

We know! He's again in safe waters—is for the moment spared! But he floats through safe waters and is again passing over the drop-off. He's floating above 250 feet of water.

Have we forgotten our golf ball? It is at the bottom of this very lake, in the deepest part, enjoying a view of a man who appears to be floating in the sky. Our golf ball has been here a dozen years and is still intact. Science won't disclose how long a golf ball may lie at the bottom of a yellow lake before ceasing to be a golf ball.

The golf ball waits forever, which is exactly what a golf ball, and everthing else, is supposed to do. Twelve years ago a man in a green sweater and yellow slacks hit the golf ball into the lake. It sank like a pearl dreaming down into oil. Soon the man in the green sweater and yellow slacks came to the high west bank and looked down. The golf ball saw absolutely no expression on his face; he appeared not at all concerned that he had hit the ball into the lake, putting it there for all time. In fact, if there was anything in the man's face it was a certain smugness, as if he could see the golf ball—*There it is,* he perhaps said to himself, and actually smiled, as if from the beginning he intended to knock the ball into the lake. He turned and left.

Teeth chattering, our golf ball poacher is floating from the safety of the drop-off into the dangerous shallows, and as we might have expected, he again puts a leg down into mud.

More desperate thrashing. And this time he is truly almost done for. He is submerged in mud.

But he swims through it—literally through the mud!—and is again in deep water. He floats on his back, breathes. He ardently whispers *Jesus*, as if He were passing by in the sky and could be hailed with a whisper.

Morning comes earlier on golf courses than anywhere else. Sportsmen love that indistinct period: hunters slip through the trees and pounce on creatures, finding in groves of gray nests so large the hunters are amazed they could have walked right up and be standing atop the thing, straddling it even, before realizing it's there, glaring up with unblinking eyes.

Of course golfers love this hour, the still fairways emerging like immense women. The earliest golfers will sometimes fling their clubs aside, kick off their shoes, and run up and down the hills.

The old groundsman in bib overalls and gray shirt watches this and no amusement or disdain shapes his cracked face as he peers from the bushes. He goes from green to green in his silent cart, turning on the sprinklers.

The groundsman tops the hill above the seventh tee and is about to widely loop the lake when he sees a naked man floating on it. *Goddamn,* the groundsman whispers.

He steers the cart down the hill, weaving through the trees that last night a certain fellow thought concealed a gang of cutthroats. He stops well short of the mud and stepping from the cart climbs the high west bank.

As he tops the bank and looks down, there is a flash—dazzling and vast, a miraculous blast of light, and the old man lifts his arm to shield his eyes and his very being, and half-turns from this angelic, explosive light.

It is the sun, of course. The groundsman moves from the high bank, and when he can look on the water, the naked man isn't there.

He couldn't have slipped away without the groundsman seeing him. There is no place he could be hiding . . . .

A pillowcase floats on the lake. Could the old man have thought *that* was a naked man?

He turns. Doesn't try to rake the pillowcase from the lake with a branch. Doesn't snag it with the telescoping golf ball-retriever floating at the edge.

He drives his cart to the seventh green, turns on the sprinklers, and listening to the spizz of water, the eager click of the nozzle heads, he gazes across the green through the sparkling diffusion of spray.

A SONG OF OLD FANGLES

He ran down the dark corridor, whizzing by rooms where people lay like stones, though surely one or two were awake to see an angelic white blur—Hobart Stull!—fly by the door. On stat calls he reached wards faster than any house orderly in the history of Wichita Falls, and so he was a great favorite with the nurses. Most orderlies on eleven-to-seven hid out and slept. But Hobart wasn't interested in sleep as such. Young, a boy practically, just married and soon to be a father, he had curly hair, blue eyes and deep dimples in both cheeks—how could the nurses resist him? And those stately, monumental nurses, big and dour as battleships, adored him, revealing glimpses of large-motioned delicacy, ponderous heavy-fleshed girlishness, and a loamy femininity that made his head spin.

For them he performed heroics, defended them and protected a disturbed patient from himself by cajoling him into handing over a butcher knife he sneaked through admission. And it was Hobart Stull the ladies called to preserve dignity when they would discover a dead person lying in a bed on their ward, as if a vulgar trick had been pulled under their noses. They became stern and silent; sometimes they were nearly addled. Only death could ripple their placid control, like a bank of revellers howling across a lake in the middle of the night.

For the nurses there was an unhinged period between the discovery of the death and when Hobart came running to perform his duty, a time when everything might come loose—the doors flapping open and beds, chairs, people sailing out like big bats. Or if nothing came undone inside, the world outside might slide away—one looked out the nearest window for reassurance that the empty street, the store fronts across the way, were still there.

By and by a doctor, half-asleep, would arrive and spend two minutes in the room with the door closed; he would come out and write on the chart. Hobart would then remove the body. But after the bed had been quickly changed and the room thoroughly cleaned, there might linger a dawnlike expectancy, for death not always left with the dead person—and once Hobart thought he heard twangy steel music from another ward, or from the roof: music jagged with distance, but persistent, chewed with fade-outs and holes of silence in which he could almost hear whispers, laughter. It wasn't until a new patient had been admitted to the room and lay in the vacant bed, that the nurses again had full control.

Even dealing with the dead was an adventure for Hobart Stull, he was that young. Of course it lacked the glory of risking a knifewound, but something in him was satisfied when he took a body to the basement morgue and lugged it from the cart onto one of the long sliding trays that he would then ease into the large refrigerator. He later recalled standing beside the body of a man he had delivered to that place. The body lay densely physical, as if the flesh had become incalculably preoccupied. Without thinking, Hobart laid his hand on the man's arm. Hobart was urging him on.

He spent most of his time from eleven to seven sitting with the nurses who last called him to their ward. They made regular rounds of their patients, and if all was quiet, between times they were free. They talked and Hobart listened, usually. Their lives were complicated, for most of them had children who were grown and married. The happiness of their children's families seemed to slip through their fingers, but they always got a good hold on the strife. The nurses accepted their children's ordeals as personal challenges, and against even the grimest, most boggling circumstances they charged into battles as dauntlessly as they would stride into a hospital room where the wolf breath of cancer hung in the air. Through the ordeals of their children's families they suffered as much as they had through their own—perhaps more, to hear them tell it. For there was just so much they could actually do. Sometimes they had to just "wait and see"—how often Hobart heard that! You might think that since they were old hands as nurses they would have realized there prevailed a downward inevitability in things, but Hobart saw in them no more acceptance or wisdom than in other people, and certainly less inclination to accepting defeat.

They were downright uncanny, sized up Hobart's moods as neatly as switching on a soap opera, and wouldn't let him be until he laid out all the trouble. Then he was counseled. Mrs. Nash was especially fine—she had a reputation even among the nurses for highpowered advice which she recited with the loveliest voice Hobart had ever heard. And she was huge. Her arms and legs bulged, and her hips were little people stowed away under her uniform, riding her through the night.

Mrs. Nash would light a cigarette, when she was sure no doctors were about and that the nurses' supervisor was off on another floor, and blowing a puff of smoke toward the low ceiling of the nursing station she would tell Hobart he shouldn't worry so much. She was sure Junie would make it through the last weeks of her pregnancy—and if Junie could, Hobart could. In fact, Mrs. Nash went on, Hobart could make it through anything! Why? "Because you're young and you're smart, Hobart," she said. "That's why."

"You're just half-right on that."

The other nurse at Mrs. Nash's station was large, though alongside Mrs. Nash she was just a rowboat. Hobart forgot nearly everything about her except there was in her family chronic strife. It clamped her in a very private silence. She had long ago refused Mrs. Nash's lyrical advice. While Mrs. Nash and Hobart talked, this other nurse stared down the dark corridor as if waiting for someone.

"No false modesty," Mrs. Nash told Hobart. "You can whip anything. You know what?"—she winked! sending shivers through him as he stared at her face, small and coy atop her big body. "I can tell about people," she said and licked her lips.

He was sure later, just as he knew it then without letting himself think about it, that he and those nurses were making love. They were doing it as thoroughly as they could under the circumstances. With her soft voice Mrs. Nash would stir and lift Hobart. She analyzed refrigerator breakdowns and debated the virtues of retred tires, as Hobart sat before her on a little stool, his knees apart, looking like frog gone a-courting, and once Mrs. Nash leaned forward, looking Hobart straight in the eye, and knocked the wind out of him by putting a hand on his knee. While she recited the log of voyages to the Salvation Army and Chester's Tenth Street Thrift Store where, she guaranteed him, a young couple could find bins of like-new baby things, her hand went higher and squeezed his thigh. Then she leaned back, lit a cigarette, and blew smoke at the ceiling.

But sometimes right in the middle of listening to Mrs. Nash or one of the others, Hobart would look away for a moment and without meaning to he would slip away and in the familiar old nervous despair he would be worrying about Junie and the pregnancy and what all that would cost, for all he had to his silly name was $16. He was always alone.

He heard nothing as Mrs. Nash talked. He had to be there in that hospital all night. Had to wait all night before he could go back out and deal with all those problems . . . No. They were worse than that. They were *enemies* that menaced what he presumptuously, innocently, with pitiful young-man naivete called his family—a seventeen-year-old child and 8/9ths of a new child, hiding from winter night in a two-room apartment in a town gouged into the prairie of North Texas, and a pick-up truck a year older than Junie, worthless old pile of iron that half the time refused to start, and a refrigerator that regularly shorted out, ruining everything, and when it wasn't playing that game it nipped Junie (never Hobart) with cunning jolts that could, all three of them knew, any day bite big enough to swallow Junie, baby, everything. And Hobart already owed going on $300 to Junie's folks, friends, uncles, Mrs. Nash. . .

And while he sat up all night there in the hospital, his problems, those hunker-shouldered cretin enemies, were resting up for another day. And when seven o'clock came and Hobart could at last go out again, they would be waiting. Full of new schemes and meanness, they would be hiding out by his truck. And Hobart would head across the parking lot, exhausted, drained out, just flat numb and vulnerable, too helpless to do anything but say *Ah hell,* as they sprang screaming and howling from their ambush and fell on him like baboons.

"I can tell about people," Mrs. Nash confided, waking him. "Even strangers. It doesn't take forever to know people, and then you see that even before you knew them they weren't really strangers." Old lover, she smiled, made him smile back.

But on Five, the top floor of the hospital, Hobart didn't make love. When he was called up there he invariably found the nurses sitting in a tense, determined silence. He soon learned this didn't mean he had stepped onto an abruptly truced battlefield. A mood prevailed on Five which wasn't directly the doing of the nurses or the patients. But on Five Hobart could feel in the air the essence of the hospital: here people who had once been well and whole were waning—some going so far they wouldn't come back. Hobart sat up there in silence with the nurses, turning when he thought he heard something over the whir of ventilation blowers and the hum of florescent lights. . .

Five dogged him, followed him home and all the way to bed where, blindfolded with one of Junie's nylons, he tossed and turned, floundering in the lapping shallows, trying to make it out to where giant fish slowly roll and glide. And often he found himself back at the hospital listening to a talking garden, row on row of nurses. He would answer them over his shoulder while he hurriedly catheterized a patch of nodding cucumbers and in the next moment he dumped a wheelbarrow of cadavers rumbling down the chute of a potato bin. He woke shouting answers to the shadows of fish big as clouds.

And in that first moment he saw too clearly and the bedroom was loud. The sun then through the curtains shriveled those moments to gray runts that edged their way to the nearest corner and disappeared. And when Hobart tried to remember what had been so clear, so urgent, he could recall nothing. Except once he woke still seeing Mrs. Nash and some nurses sitting at the station on Five. In the rooms along the hall patients patted air. "They're finishing off," Mrs. Nash said, smiling coyly. The patients sank away, receding farther and farther into their rooms. "What is it now?" Hobart asked. "They're going off," she said, "to wide fields where there are no people and no familiar things."

And Junie burst into the room. "It's time!"

Hobart leaped from bed and stumbled around the room trying to find the door of the hospital. Junie jerked the stocking from his head and he got his pants on and a shirt, ran out and the truck amazingly started right up, and he drove Junie to the hospital. An orderly whisked her up to O.B., and Hobart went to the waiting room.

He paced and faunched for a couple of hours but had to sit down. He sat straight as a board, but he slept. They were in a bus station, there was no time to waste. Hobart was looking for Junie and at the same time talking to a young man who was following him around. The young man was Hobart's son!

Junie had no trouble delivering an eight-pound boy. They named him Hobart Stull, Jr. But a few months later Junie said he should have been named Dick Bunch, Jr. Hobart thought it over and decided he could live with that. But Junie couldn't. After she left, Hobart quit his job at the hospital, waited around a few weeks, and then left Wichita Falls. He set out to do a good job of turning over a leaf.

SELLING

My product was slow in catching on, so the severest economies were necessary: I traveled by train instead of flying, and at least three nights a week I was en route, bobbing and tilting among jumbled dreams that permitted me at best only halfway into sleep; but I saved even more money by sparing myself the expense of a hotel room. My office was my suitcase, my factory the basement of an empty house in Sheboygan where I manufactured the Hobart Stull All-Purpose Frog Lock. I called it that not because it locked frogs, but because if my invention shared a resemblance with anything under the sun it was with the frog, and though it wasn't truly all-purpose (it could lock only filing cabinets with 100% efficiency, but it also locked rather snugly certain models of the Gossman refrigerator, a brand being made at that time in El Paso), there was something intriguing about the name; by phone I could capture the imagination of potential buyers, and often I sold orders for the lock, sight unseen, just on the name!

I researched several hemispheres of the business world and found that roughly 60% of all filing cabinets were of the unlockable sort; further research hinted (hinted, indeed. It blared it unequivocally!) that in your average large city more filing cabinets lurked in the corners of otherwise vacant rooms, than the city's combined population of men, women, children, dogs, and cats. My dreams were crowded with filing cabinets, their unlocked drawers wobbling open as my train went through the night.

In my way I was successful: businessmen took to me from the first hello, and would talk to me for hours. I didn't understand this affinity, and don't to this day. They even called me long distance, but phone conferences weren't the same as face-to-face, and they would end insisting that I rush right over. I would hop a night train and arrive (crumpled but willing) for a morning conference that likely as not would last into the afternoon, my clients* and I talking and riding taxis about town to the offices of their friends, who soon became my close friends as well and potential customers for my locks. I was in demand to lecture the sales force and office staffs of companies large and small, and at least once a week I spoke to business clubs on up-beat salesmanship, tact, and self-awareness in the field. The fee I received was usually adequate to cover my train fare, with enough left over for a sandwich and a candy bar from the vendor who went from car to car as the train rattled along.

I slowly realized I lacked true dedication to the frog lock, and that my attitude toward money as such was all wrong: I was in other words out for the friends and the train rides, just as I had in my younger days taken so keenly to being a hospital orderly for the opportunity of running down dark halls in the middle of the night, and of sitting around talking to nurses. The camaraderie of salesmen was an inestimable pleasure, and the special satisfaction I derived from the trainrides were, and remain, impossible for me to either understand or accurately describe: I was never so content as when I was riding through the dark. But it was more than that—and less. For those trips weren't journeys into big, expansive night; rather, they were retracings of the same deep experience, the somehow private night in which things seldom seriously changed. I made the same trips so often I had an indelible familiarity with each mile of the way and every shadow that moved in the business of the night. Drowsing by the window I watched the flow of moon-dim landscapes and

*I won't go on and on about these fellows, fine and fascinating individuals though they were. The names of a few, and a daub here and there, should suffice: Max Dellert, attorney at law, whose hobby was large yellow hats; George Daah, manufacturer of the three-wheeled automobile, the Marmaduke; Lester McKeynough, manager of Cavanaugh's Convalescent Retreat and Restorium; Russell Doister, president of the Effingham Elks Club and husband of the stunning Miss Illinois, 1956, Rosemarie Whumlur Doister; Cecil Dare, retired mail clerk, whose hobby was oriental novelties.

processions of lordly trees; small towns of shadows clumped together—vague houses, leaning barns, and as we blundered through New Harmony, Indiana at three o'clock one morning I looked out and saw a cow standing on a street corner. I learned those little towns by heart, thousands of them: a long wall lit by three umbrellas of gray light from three streetlamps; in another town a streetlamp calling partway from dark a lane where the same two cars were always parked on the same side of the road, across from the same pick-up truck that seemed each time to have sunk deeper in its place.

Once I woke convinced I was on the wrong train, hurrying in the wrong direction. And each moment the train was sliding farther North like a silk hankerchief slipping over the edge of a table. Even after I reassured myself that I was on the right train, I felt a peculiar anxiety. I looked around. The car was brownish-yellow and dim. The faces of the other passengers, only a handful, were dark as they slept, their heads nodding, their expressions sour and sagging as the train jiggled their faces farther and farther out of shape—by dawn when they woke they wouldn't recognize themselves and would have to catch the first train back to look for themselves along the way. I had no way of knowing, but I felt certain these weren't the same people who were on the train when I boarded. I sat back and made myself close my eyes. Sleep was usually the answer. I was getting older, needed to develop a proper attitude toward sleep. I didn't pass off but opened my eyes just in time to duck what I thought was a huge bird swooping low over the seats.

Of course it wasn't a bird, but a person coming down the aisle at a dead run. The person stopped short and took a seat across the aisle. She was a small narrow-faced woman wearing brown. You were talking out loud in your sleep, I thought she said: her lips moved and I lipread this; if she actually spoke aloud it was much too softly for me to hear over the noise of the train. "No I wasn't," I said in spite of myself. I didn't want to talk to her, for I suddenly realized I was exhausted and needed to be alone.

"Yes you were. I heard you," she said. Her face was indistinct. I decided something was wrong with the lighting in the car. Then her face seemed to move and I took it for a smile.

I turned and looked out the window—and again for a moment I felt we were northbound. Then it struck me that my success and pleasure during the day was from now on to be counterbalanced and negated by awful ordeals on these night trains; I would have to suffer nights in equal proportion to the pleasure of my days. I believed I understood: from now on, every morning between three and four-thirty I would get the works—dread and people would around me blossom like toadstools while I sat and watched.

In the black mirror of the window I saw the woman standing in the aisle, leaning toward me, a large object in her hands. I turned and she sat in the seat beside me. The object was a large black book, a photograph album. She slipped out a picture, held it up with the fingertips of both hands. I looked at it. People. Tiny dim things that I *assumed* were people. They stood in front of old houses. I looked up at the woman's dark face. She was oddly attractive, but perhaps that was only because she was so near me and I was so exhausted; in a group of people she would have quickly faded to invisibility. It is likely she could only be seen when no one else was around, and the family in the pictures in her album also tended to disappear: in the light of day if one looked into the album (if he could find it) the pictures would show only houses, open doors and empty lawns, vacant porch swings.

She was speaking. ". . . and by then of course we were ready to move anywhere. When you are finally ready to go, you will go anywhere." She took out another picture and held it for me to see. I looked: little people.

She went on as if we were old acquaintances, and I tried to see her more clearly, her thin, brownish-yellow face: perhaps we had met through business, or maybe like me she often rode this train and we had seen each other without really seeing each other. Or had she and I known each other years ago—perhaps she had been a patient at the hospital where I worked, or maybe she had been a nurse on the day shift. I leaned still closer, as if to better see the next photo she held, but instead I looked straight into her face. It was awful. She was suffering, her mouth a slit. And in spite of the severity, the fierceness, in that lucidity just prior to knowing her I saw the child she had been, the little girl grown and gone off to ride trains and dedicate her nights to the photographs of this family, these little people who at least for a while weren't lost. Of course I loved her, with all her terror and anxiety, her smell of basement and old clothes.

"Do you like it?" she said, looking up.

"The pictures? Well . . . yes. I suppose I do."

"Good." She closed the album on her knees and reached down for her purse. She dug into it and got a wooden box. She undid the little brass latch and took from the box a pen and an inkwell no bigger than a thimble. Carefully she opened the inkwell, dipped in the pen, and looked at me. "What is your name?"

I told her, and asked hers.

She didn't answer, but wrote *Hobart Stull* in gold across the frayed cover of the album.

"It's yours." She smiled rather smugly and put the pen and ink back into their box. "Only ten dollars and ninety-five cents."

"Oh. The old mazuma." I stared at my name on the album. "That's not so bad, ten ninety-five. Only problem is, I have only. . ." I took out my coin purse, unsnapped it, and spilled out the money into my hand. She and I counted it at a glance. "Thirty-five cents."

I looked up at her and couldn't read her expression—except I saw she wasn't exactly enthusiastic. But on the other hand she didn't appear disappointed.

"Tell you what I'll do," I said. I put my money away and leaning down I pulled my satchel from under my seat and opened it. There was my sales array—an army of staunch frog locks poised ready to hop into the fray and secure the world's loose ends. "I'll give you some of these for the album." She took one and looked it over. We tried it on the photo album and found it not wholly effective as a book lock, though part of the failure lay in the fact that the frayed cover of the album was too soft for the lock to get a good bite.

I started giving her the locks and she stuck them in her pockets and piled them on her lap, and while we were doing this, a little girl appeared beside us, smiling with feverish brightness, her eyes so eager, so urgent, surely she was straining herself. Her hair was golden and a-swarm with curls so tight it occurred to me the child was somehow clenching her scalp. She wore a pink dress, brittle with starch, that showed her long and skinny, blazing white legs and her stick-like arms. She winked at me!

"This is Rundella, my little girl," the woman said.

"Okay?" Rundella said.

"Hit it," the woman said.

Rundella tapdanced in the aisle, swinging her arms, leaning forward and smiling her marvelous, frightening smile, while her shoes hammered the floor. I grinned like an idiot and nodded encouragement which she hardly needed, and she danced on and on. Her face was soon quite flushed and perspiring, but she continued. The other passengers gathered around, some smiling, others staring blankly, watching Rundella and glancing at her mother who hooked her arm through mine and snuggled against me. Rundella danced on indefatigably, and the people leaned on the seats, some with their eyes nearly closed though they seemed determined to stay for all of Rundella's dance, and when it seemed the child would collapse or perhaps explode, she slowed her tempo to an even sturdier rhythm and began singing! Of course she was quite out of breath, but she managed a pretty fair rendition of "Way Down Upon the Suwanee River," followed by "Light My Fire," and ending with a rousing version of "On The Road to Mandalay," and all of us joined her on the chorus as she swung her little arms and marched in place.

At last Rundella stopped and, gasping for breath, sat down right on the floor. The other passengers began humming an old song. I leaned back, relieved that the child's heart hadn't burst, and my companion leaned her head on my shoulder and spoke softly, making plans. I grunted approval as she talked, but I really didn't need to say a word: the elaborate plans included a long journey (the continuation, I supposed, of this one) that would end in a small town in the West. There would be plenty to do, and there would be, as she put it, "all the people we'll need."

It made sense. I looked out the window and saw the first marks of dawn. When I turned back, opening my eyes, it was day. The train rattled loudly, with much rocking and leaning. The car was empty except for one other passenger. At the end of the car an old man sat with his hat pushed forward over his eyes.

At my destination I was getting my things together and saw on the dirty floor the torn corner of a photograph under my seat. As I put on my overcoat I nudged the scrap of paper with the toe of my shoe. There was darkness, perhaps a tree; above and beyond that there was a white triangle, perhaps the sky.

THE IDOLS OF AFTERNOON

On different days of the month the West Frankfort Rotary, Elks, and Moose met at the Downtowner Hotel where they had lunch and over coffee and cigars listened to speakers tell of their travels, or their acquaintance with famous people, or their power of memory.

With the dour vagueness of old hotels, the Buckner stared across the town square at the doings at the Downtowner. In better days Abraham Lincoln stopped over at the Buckner, or so it was said, and a week after his death he began roaming the halls and rattling doorknobs. You weren't a regular at the Buckner until you heard his heavy tread or woke to his fumbling at your door—though if you were a regular you knew the footsteps were likely those of two widows who lived on the second floor. Square-shouldered and tall, they looked like old men in big gingham dresses, for life had duped them at the end, thickened them, solidified them, and led the poor things off into a muddled, shadowy sort of manhood. The two old widows were heard but seldom seen about the hotel, and when seen they would be fading down a hall or turning a corner.

When Miss Eula Kirk's heart gave out, she retired, left St. Louis, and came home to West Frankfort. She stayed at the Buckner, planning to find a room in a private home; surely a nice widow lady or an older couple wouldn't mind taking in a quiet roomer who sewed. But the window in Eula's room at the Buckner looked down on a side street that was never busy, and the hotel's comfortable brown silence, as if it were always late afternoon, held Eula. She felt peculiarly content at the hotel. One night she woke and heard the floor creak outside her door. The next day as she went down to the lobby she stopped and, staring through the still air, suddenly expected to see her father, long dead, walk through the front door and head for the cigar counter.

When Eula met Miss Smight, the matter was settled; she would stay on at the Buckner.

Miss Smight had a two-room suite, and each afternoon she and Eula talked in the sitting room, a small hexagonal room with walls slanting to a ceiling smaller than the floor and tending to lean the ladies forward and make them whisper. Eula's favorite place was a love seat facing Miss Smight's large chair by the window, where early afternoons framed Miss Smight with white that sank gradually to yellow.

Miss Smight loved dark blue organdy; it rustled eagerly as she leaned to the side, her chair straining, and crossed her legs. Though not fat, Miss Smight was certainly stately and wore on her amazingly large face—the largest Eula had ever seen, and the most beautiful—white powder, very much, and bright red lipstick.

As they talked Miss Smight sometimes assumed a rather plangent expression and, tilting, paused as an intriguing murmur came from within the organdy. At first this mystified Eula, but she caught on and if she happened to be speaking as Miss Smight began her tilt, Eula would stop so the muffled comment could be heard.

Many nights Eula lay awake in her own narrow room, going over their conversations, her eyes wide in the darkness and seeing her friend's big face which seemed always to be smiling in a special way just beyond what was being said and just beyond Eula's grasp. Once Eula was still awake when the slow, suspicious gray of dawn entered the hotel and stirred the two old widows onto a prowl—or maybe it was Lincoln, for the footsteps were heavy and urgent. As if she had been waiting for him to come, Eula slipped off to sleep, where she went running barefooted down a dirt road. Suddenly there came a fog and then she saw Miss Smight at the side of the road. She had been waiting for Eula!

In their afternoon conversations Eula didn't mention the sounds, but once she and Miss Smight were interrupted by muttering in the hall. And the door jarred, but didn't open. "Who is that?" Eula whispered to Miss Smight.

She smiled. "Them!"

"Oh." Eula assumed she meant the widows, for one evening Eula had seen them in the distance looking at her over their shoulders. "Have they always been here at the hotel?"

"They came after me."

"It's nice they have each other."

Miss Smight took a handkerchief from her sleeve and putting it to her lips whispered through it: "If people knew what goes on, there would be a scandal. People would say it's naughty." Miss Smight laughed, her voice quite deep. "Would you?"

"It would depend."

"Indeed." Lowering the handkerchief, Miss Smight fanned herself and said softly, "It would depend on whether you like a little naughtiness now and then."

Eula felt herself blushing, and again Miss Smight laughed.

That Saturday they strolled around the square. Tuesday Eula and Miss Smight listened to the band in the pavilion. Later in the week they drove in Miss Smight's Hudson to a shopping center at the edge of town, returning to the hotel exhausted but excited. And Eula sat down and without knowing she was going to, talked at great length about her bosses and the seamstresses in the shop where she had worked for forty-three years—the squibble-squabbles and fights, the time Earline Griggs was gone two weeks and came back without saying a word as if she hadn't missed a day, and the time they found a dead bum in the alley behind the shop . . .

Eula talked faster and faster. She remembered when Mr. McShane fired Mavis Coy for putting a dead mouse in his lunch pail, though he hired her back the next day. And she remembered when little Eula Kirk, just a girl, started work. During her first week in the shop she happened to be in the toilet when Mr. McShane, who had been working two days trying to fix a sewing machine, came in carrying it over his head, his face red and his eyes bulging. "Out of the way!" he roared. Eula hopped up and Mr. McShane slammed the sewing machine into the commode.

Eula talked all afternoon and the next day. But when she went to Miss Smight's the third day and they were seated, nothing came. "Well," Eula said. She gave a little laugh. "Well, I guess . . . " Suddenly burning as if she would cry, she took a deep breath and held it.

Miss Smight said, "While you were there, I stayed in West Frankfort." Miss Smight's face was expressionless under all its powder. "I could go, and you could stay here . . . " She lifted a hand and turned it palm-up as if it would be equally easy, a gesture of air, to unlive lives and set forth again.

Oh no, Eula almost said. For she already felt she had lost everything—and, even worse, Eula heard crass little voices laughing inside herself, and, like a naked boy dancing around her, the thought taunted her that she had lost nothing, that not a day, not one minute of it, had been worth keeping.

Miss Smight took Eula's arm and led her from the room and the hotel. She walked Eula around the town square, pausing before store windows, and Eula saw her own and Miss Smight's reflections and beyond them the mannequins, and beyond them, very far away, like tumbling mounds of shadow, people shopping in the stores.

They returned to the hotel and in the sitting room, with the window yellow behind her, Miss Smight began a story about something that happened to her. Eula cried as soon as Miss Smight started and kept saying, "You poor thing. You poor, poor thing," and as she cried harder, everything swam together in that vague air which seems to prevail—and Eula saw herself and Miss Smight looking in store windows, their faces blank and owly. Then people came by and looked in at Eula and Miss Smight who sat motionless inside a window.

When Eula stopped crying she was startled to see that Miss Smight hadn't also cried. Her great white face was as placid as ever; moreover, her lips were lifted in a rather sly smile.

The next day Eula knocked and Miss Smight called out for her to enter, but she wasn't in the sitting room when Eula went in and sat down. She waited, staring at the door to the other room. Then it opened and Miss Smight made her entrance. She wasn't wearing organdy, but a tight-fitting silk dress, dark green and shiny like the skin of some great sleek beast. She stood before Eula, an imperiously bland expression on her face.

Eula sat with her mouth open, her face burning. She turned and looked up, as if for a way to the ceiling.

"Well?" Miss Smight said softly. "How do you like it?"

"I don't."

Miss Smight sat in her chair before the window, and they were silent, Eula refusing to look at her. Then Eula heard a steady, dulcet clicking. And though she tried to resist, she looked . . .

Smiling, Miss Smight fingered a strand of big black beads around her neck. She spoke.

Eula refused to listen. But in spite of herself—maybe it was those beads, clicking cozily—Eula listened as Miss Smight talked about Jasper Satin of Wichita Falls, Texas. "So manly," Miss Smight said. "And frisky."

Eula stared into the beads and, not intending to, said in a petulant, helpless whisper, "Why . . . ?" She couldn't say the rest, couldn't ask why of all words Miss Smight had turned loose those, for inside Eula they jiggled forth the awesome concept of manly friskiness!—and Eula realized she had been ignorant of something vast. It was as if she had lived all these years without knowing there was yet another state in the Union, one where there was always a lot happening, and which people only talked about in secret.

Miss Smight was silent. "Well?" Eula said, her teeth clenched.

"Well, my goodness," Miss Smight said and, looking down, succeeded in smiling shyly.

"Did you and this Jasper Satin fall in love?"

"Did we fall in love?" Miss Smight fairly crowed with laughter, and tilting to the side, crossed her legs and beneath the smooth slide of silk there stirred a mirthful and rather loud murmur. "Love barely describes it."

The next day there was Owen Wiggler of Duquoin, Illinois, a horseman . . .

And that—*horseman*—had odd force, stunning Eula as if air had grabbed itself into a fist and socked her into a float across the bottomlands of Southern Illinois, where horses splashed through creeks and up muddy banks . . .

"Owen Wiggler was a small man and—" Miss Smight paused, smiling in that sly, special way, "I never knew what to expect." Of course! Eula realized all at once how fascinating small men were. Quick—and unpredictable! "Owen Wiggler took me to the horse shows," Miss Smight said.

Eula sank back and put her cheek to her shoulder. Owen Wiggler, small and rigidly straight, walks arm in arm with Miss Smight, taking her to a horse show . . . "Those at night were best," Miss Smight said. Of course they were, because they were under torchlight. Eula sees torchlight glinting on sleek horses like fire under water, as they are led by small men with muscular arms and cunning hands. The horses stride smoothly, their heads nodding in that elegant agreement of walking horses . . .

Whispering, Miss Smight described the prizes, and though Eula listened intently, everything receded, falling into her like stars from a black sky. Alone, Eula Kirk whispers *Prizes* and is off to distant fairgrounds, *Prizes* lifting her lips as she whispers it again, kissing air.

The next afternoon when Eula was in her chair and ready, Miss Smight said, "Keg Jamaket hurt me."

"Oh." Eula breathed levelly once, twice. "What happened?"

Miss Smight lifted a hand. "My thumb." The thumb pointed to the ceiling. "And he hurt me here—" Smiling archly, she turned in the chair, reached under her arm, and ran her hand down her ribs. "And here—" She tapped her thumb on one breast, then the other. "And here—" as Eula closed her eyes. "And here . . . "

Eula sees a woods sunk in watery grayness, and then a young woman, tall and straight, in a white dress, pauses astride a log, then steps over it and walks swiftly, almost defiantly, through the woods, and a little woman hurries after her. The girl stops, and the little woman too, and Eula listens with them. Nothing. Then the wan, complex song of birds. And beneath that a distant mutter, like the first vague voice of intention, a burring sigh, that as the girl and the little woman move on, becomes distinguishable as the rasping of a saw. The girl runs . . .

"He was in a thicket," Miss Smight said. "He jumped out and grabbed me. 'Keg Jamaket, you leave me alone,' I told him. But he held me and kissed me and pushed me down . . . "

Eula can't see them. She again hears the saw grinning its vicious glee through wood. It slows; the sound fades. A wind moves through the woods like a great animal leaning from the sky, bending the trees as it lies down. The wind dies and the sitting room is tight with silence. Eula sees them, and it is not as Miss Smight said, not at all.

Keg Jamaket in overalls stands against a tree. Slowly a long arm swings up, with a very large hand at the end of it, and the girl in white steps forward and with both hands she takes it, one hand grasping his big thumb.

Squinting, Eula squeezes the gray woods tight and turns it on end: Miss Smight's words sink, clopping deep into the woods, a garble of stones dropped in an empty well. Eula listens to her own breathing, stentorian, monstrous.

But she is with them again, standing against the girl's back, her chin dug into the girl's shoulder and looking with her into Keg Jamaket's flat face. His eyes are big and perfectly round and set far apart. His ears tuck neatly against his head. "His cheeks were so smooth," Eula hears. And Eula sees they are. Then everything is gone.

After a long wait Eula opened her eyes. The yellow window framed Miss Smight, and Eula couldn't see her face. Perhaps a corona was drawing Miss Smight out the window and into the sky. Or Miss Smight was drawing the sky down onto her, bringing it on the huge wings of surprise into the room to lay on Eula's lap.

That night dogs came loping out of ravines in the walls, and Eula kept talking—it was her only hope. She talked faster and faster, not hearing a word, and then woke as she was tiptoeing down the hall. At the stairs she stared into the lobby. The old, high-backed chairs gaped at the lobby reflected in the smooth black front windows, beyond which was framed the street and town square, an old gray picture. Eula turned and calmly followed herself down the hall to Miss Smight's door, which was locked, of course. On the other side was the sun shining, and did Miss Smight sit by the window, whispering to the room? Then Eula was again in her own bed, suddenly awake and hearing *her* door rattling, followed by those familiar hurried footsteps passing as dawn shrank her room still narrower.

She refused to go to Miss Smight's that afternoon, and the next day Eula left the hotel and walked down a tree-lined street to a house where several little women came to the windows and looked out. She went up to the door and was admitted. Eula was at the Eastern Star. The ladies sat in a circle in the living room and talked four hours. When Eula left, she walked up the street and, reaching the town square, stared across at the Buckner, its windows blazing red in the late afternoon sun.

"It was so nice," Eula said, "and they're all just wonderful. I know you'll love it. We will go every afternoon . . . "

Looking into the light, Eula couldn't clearly see Miss Smight's face, but it seemed even larger than before, as if time, alone with her, had pressed especially hard against her face, pushing her deeper into herself. And Miss Smight sat with her eyes closed. Had she fallen asleep? Or . . . No—for at that moment she nodded and spoke.

But not to Eula. She spoke over her shoulder to the window, the sky. "You just wouldn't believe it."

"I'll believe it," Eula quickly said. "I'm sure I will."

"Charlie?" Miss Smight said as she turned to the room.

Eula glanced at the door to the other room, then along the walls to the hall door. Eula whispered, "Who is he?"

Miss Smight closed her eyes. "Why, he is Charlie Leonard. Men come miles to see him. He . . ." She opened her eyes and turned, whispering, "Charlie?" and as she looked out the window, Eula said, "I see them." Eula sees two men walking down a dirt street—and, walking the other direction, a little woman who stops as they pass, and turns and follows them. They come to a large house where several men sit on the front porch smoking their pipes. A man stands before them, his hands on his hips, talking. "There's Charlie," Miss Smight says. But the house, the street, slipped into a wall.

Eula waited, but it wouldn't return. Miss Smight sat with her head cocked to the side. Eula said, "How long did . . . ?"

Miss Smight laughed and sat back. "I have no idea." Of course not. Eula understood perfectly—for now when she tried to think of things that happened a month ago, or a week, or even yesterday, a turn in the corridor brought her to a wall without a door. "You had Charlie Leonard for years and years, didn't you?" Eula said. "Even when you were old."

Miss Smight's expression grew pensive. She nodded carefully.

Eula crosses the porch and steps through the front door into the living room, as big as the Buckner's lobby, with a wide staircase like the Buckner's, and she knows there are just as many rooms upstairs, if not more, all with little ceilings, and through each room winds the same faded carpet with its subtle, purple vine which Eula has traced so often, deciphering its loops and convolutions.

Miss Smight and Eula sit on the sofa in the living room, and a door opens. Charlie Leonard enters wearing a black coat and a big hat. Taking off his hat, he speaks to Miss Smight, though Eula can't hear. As they talk, a pale young man steps from behind Charlie Leonard.

And then another, who isn't wearing a shirt–his chest pale and bony–and then another young man steps forth, and another . . .

Charlie Leonard crosses the room, shaking the floor, to the sofa and stands squarely before Miss Smight. Eula sees his face: a coarse chin, bent nose, and heavy-lidded eyes that are certain and bright. Eula is afraid Charlie Leonard will strike Miss Smight, for he stands looking down at her cruelly. Then Miss Smight amazes Eula. She glances at Eula, winks, then turns and, reaching out, Miss Smight sews a big gold button on Charlie Leonard's trousers.

The young men, all of them shirtless now, crowd around. "What about all the young men?" Eula says.

Miss Smight laughs. "Oh my, yes. The boys. We can't forget the boys." In a yellow room Eula sees Miss Smight slowly lying down, her great white body rolling on itself like cumulus clouds, and a young man springs forward, a javelin, and is lost in her. "The old men," Eula says.

Miss Smight moans. "My oh my, how they loved it, coming home to mama." Miss Smight, large and wearing pale blue organdy, kneels before an old man who sits on the side of a bed, his hands on his knees, looking down at her and talking. He lifts a hand, dark and huge, a wedge, and puts it on Miss Smight's shoulder as she pulls off one of his shoes.

A young man, then another, playing chase through the hotel, burst into the sitting room and out the other door. Another runs in and stops. With his eyes big, intent, he takes off his clothes. "Touch him and you burn your hand," Miss Smight whispers. Eula feels his blood pouring through him like fire. Eula runs her hand along the shoulder of an old man, smooth and cool. Eula goes down the hall to the open door of another room and sees a skinny boy, big-eyed and almost scared, drop his overalls and glide across Miss Smight. Far down the hall Eula hears Miss Smight laugh. Then she hears Miss Smight whispering, her head beside hers on the pillow in Eula's bed: "Sweet. So sweet." Eula licks the boy's shoulder, a big warm apple, the sun burning deep inside it. His stomach is flat and smooth.

Eula turns on her side and he isn't there. By the special, dense darkness in the window she knows this is that long moment in which night ends, and as she knew she would she hears the old boards groan under the carpet in the hall and as her window and the room lift in the stern opacity of dawn, he stops at her door and finds it wide open. Without hesitating, he enters, and he is taller than Charlie Leonard, taller than any man Eula has ever seen. He goes to the window and stands with his back to Eula. At last he turns and walks to her bed. He leans down, his chest and shoulders and head becoming larger and larger, a huge tree, its limbs widening to all the sky, and she wonders if he will ever reach her—and thinking that, she loses wondering and becomes the night left behind, smoothly and easily a part of his descending. She takes a deep breath as she realizes his falling will take forever.

THE HEART OF LOVINGKIND

The first forty-odd years of Ernie's life were spent in a melancholy resulting from his grief and feeling of loss over the beautiful love his Uncle Bob somehow perverted, thus bringing about his untimely end. Edith killed Uncle Bob after they had been together for years. She stomped him. Neighbors in nearby trailers heard the noise; it kept waking them all night. But they later told the police they hadn't been suspicious. Irritated yes—but not suspicious. For Bob and Edith often trained nights—sometimes all night. Ernie decided that was probably why Edith killed Bob. Bob kept her in the boxing ring all day, and when she wasn't boxing, Bob made her perform her standing backflip and other leaps. And then likely as not they trained all night. So poor, gentle Edith, giving in to despair, killed the man she loved.

But their life together hadn't always been so desperate. Ernie recalled Bob and Edith's happier times; in his youth Ernie had spent a day now and then with them when they were touring with the Sammers Shows, before Bob started losing control to brandy. What caused Bob to drink more and more? Ernie often wondered. Was it guilt? Or drab loneliness, which Ernie, all these years a bachelor, knew so well? Though Bob had Edith all along. He couldn't have been *very* lonely—the two of them in that trailer. Ernie remembered well those visits, he relived them often: the three of them sitting in the tiny trailer, Bob smoking his pipe and talking of his youth in Vancouver, Edith demurely sipping from her bowl of tea, now and then glancing across at Ernie.

Looking back at those quiet evenings, Ernie decided Edith's wan glances across the table were the beginning of his own loneliness—a strange loneliness not unlike that which sent his Uncle Bob to the grave.

Ernie was doing fairly well in used cars, staying sober enough, and wandering through one romance after another, for he was handsome in a plump, round-faced, cherubic way: women of all sorts found themselves standing before him, looking into his almond-shaped eyes and wondering what it was that pulled them to him. And Ernie had no idea and wasn't particularly interested in either his magnetic powers or the women they worked upon—though on several occasions he was nearly married before he asked himself the crucial question *But why*? Upon which he would turn and, to the dismay of those counting on him, walk away.

Currently he was courting, in a sense, Margaret Tutzlav. She had passed the lot on Houpton Road one day, bought a mangled Morris, and—as Margaret would say—what is *much* much more, she came into the acquaintance of her dear Mr. Seervus—which she always called Ernie. They took infrequent weekend trips to the coast. Margaret was large, dowdy, inclined to fuzziness: little wool worms strayed in her tufty reddish hair which reminded Ernie, in spite of himself, of Edith's; and Margaret had a dry, faded complexion that an hour after she returned, red and robust, from a hike on the beach, was again rather gray. She was well past forty, but she told Ernie, hoping he would find it worthy news, both her older sisters, and her mother as well, had stopped aging once they turned fifty—that from fifty to eighty they hadn't changed one smitch.

And that *was* worthy news, Ernie supposed. For his part, there was his father, a stout chap who still worked a full day at the mill when he chose, and claimed that he went once a month to the Red Cock, a crossroads gehenna. And there had been Uncle Bob. . . "Tell me something about that one," Margaret urged. "You always just mention him and then clam up."

"There's nothing to tell. That's all."

"Ah. One of those. Every family has one. Ours was my cousin, Wallace Turgin. No one ever told me the full on him, but I suspect he was girlish."

Ernie sighed.

And his life went on. Then late one afternoon, while standing on the lot in the rain, looking down Houpton Road, where there were some factories, some grubby shops and a pub or two burrowed among rows of gray stone buildings, Ernie's thoughts were taking their usual melancholy route: he was anticipating the time when he would fall ill and the doctor would shake his head and mildly inform Ernie that it was tuberculosis of the extremities, or cancer of the spleen, or. . . And then into Ernie's field of vision appeared, as if from heaven, the perfectly oval and radiant face of Miss Pearl Fish. She pretended to be interested in the '57 Oldsmobile, but she quickly let it be known that she was truly interested in photographing him. Pearl was a devotee of the ovoid—she didn't hesitate to tell Ernie that was what most attracted her to him, as she crept among the dripping hulks on the car lot: looking up through her camera she saw a sublime oval standing with his back to her.

Aggressively cheerful, Pearl was short, rather stocky but attractive in an athletic, vigorously alert way. Though she was dependably merry and bright, with the high spirits that come from good health and a powerful will, Ernie perceived that if she were ever crossed or done a disservice, she would be a dauntless, indeed formidable, foe. Not that Ernie planned any disservices for Pearl. Readily he was quite fond of her, with her soft brown hair, her round cheeks, and her habit, when concentrating on her photography or her sketchbook, of pursing her lips into a perfect, plump heart.

They dined together that evening—Pearl picking up the tab with a delighted trill—and the evening ended with the two of them sipping cognac in the stainless steel and marble elegance of her town flat, surrounded by ovoid sculpture large and small. That weekend Pearl planned an outing—a weekend in the country at her home near Snell, a village to the north. Ernie could meet Pearl's mother, Athena Fish.

The country home, Rounsmeer, was a mansion set far back from the narrow road, and nearly completely hidden by huge trees, tidy thickets, hedges, and bushes rambling around a large, egg-shaped pond. Before they even reached the house, Pearl stopped the car in the driveway. She had Ernie put on a broad-brimmed white hat and pose by the pond where she took numerous shots with her camera, while white geese ambled over to have a look. Then on to the house and Athena Fish—a tall, gray lady with a narrow, icy face and large, square eye sockets hiding gray eyes which, when Mrs. Fish was excited, shone with cold, electric intensity.

Drinks were served in a huge room crowded with grand furniture multiplied tenfold by mirrors lining the walls. Ernie sat back, after his third cocktail, enjoying the strange peace and quietude of Rounsmeer: it was quite like moving away in time.

And that impression had no sooner passed through his mind than Athena Fish leaned forward and said, "The Fishes have been important in our history."

Ernie nodded to that, though he felt it was a rather aimless observation unless the good lady's hobby was evolution. Then he realized she referred to her family.

"The name Seervus. . .?" Mrs. Fish inquired. "What might that be?"

"Roman," Pearl shot in brightly.

"Indeed!"

"And I love it," Pearl said. "It has such a perfect oval sound. *Seeeer*vus." She looked at Ernie with twinkling eyes. Ernie smiled at her, sipped his drink, and they listened while Athena related a few glories of the past. As the afternoon faded into dusk, Ernie slipped off into one of his mildly abject reveries, gazing out the window and into his own past, while Pearl sat off to the side, sketching Ernie in a large sketchbook, ripping out page after page as she worked away. Out the window Ernie looked down the expanse of the yard toward the pond. The last rays of sunset, like an aureole beach on the ocean of space, melted the time-blurred window panes to amber sand. And then suddenly Ernie saw bobbing by the window an unmistakable form: narrow head, forward leaning, intent, with pointy ears, slender neck and narrow shoulders: *kangaroo.*

Ernie gasped—and quickly covered it with a cough and a manly *harumph.* His eyes misting, he shook his head sadly, knowing this would have happened inevitably; he merely marveled that the hallucinations should start now of all times.

And as this was straying across his mind, Pearl pealed forth, "Gigi!" She sprang from her chair, ran to the French doors, and pushed them open.

With a smooth gliding bound, in came Gigi, her forelegs reached out to Pearl. As they embraced, there was an extremely long moment, a fatal moment, when Gigi looked over Pearl's shoulder and met the eyes of Ernie.

They stared at each other for what in slow amber time was an endless period, a brilliant cascade of millennia, and what Ernie saw in Gigi's eyes was an answer—rather coy, but rather serious.

Following their short honeymoon—a week in Amsterdam, Pearl sketching Henry Moore sculptures in the museum—Ernie and Pearl settled into a breezy, frivolous routine that caused in Ernie, after twenty years of a bludgeoning existence, ten to fourteen hours a day selling iron, a fine giddiness—as if he were no longer bound by gravity, as if he could at will float with gentle billowing bounds wherever he pleased, whenever he pleased. He didn't sell the lot and the seven or eight (already he had forgotten how many) cars on it; he simply didn't go back. In amber dreams he willed the cars to slowly sink into the mud of Houpton Road, where, in his dreams, it always rained.

He went during the week into the city with Pearl, who rushed about, very busy with her camera, her sketches, sculpture, and other projects. They drove out for weekends with Athena, who, Pearl confided to Ernie one night, didn't have much time left. "And when she passes?" Ernie inquired, his heart beating rather fast.

"Why. . . What do you mean, Ernie love?"

"What do we do with Rounsmeer?"

"Why, I suppose we dump it. After all, it's pretty useless as far as I'm concerned." She meant the photography and the art. She had shot and sketched Rounsmeer for years: she had used it up.

"I rather like the old place," Ernie said.

She detected the quaver in his voice. "I believe you *do.* You're just like old Roy"—her father. "Then we'll keep it. For you. I must tell Athena. She'll be overjoyed that we're going to keep Rounsmeer after she's gone."

"But don't you think we're counting the chicken before. . ."

"On no, Ernie love. Dear Athena, I'm afraid, has just the least bit of time left." She paused, then, "There, there, Ernie. We mustn't take it too hard. The poor dear *has* had a full life. I'm confident she's ready."

While Ernie's face streamed with tears of joy, his sobbing, which became quite violent, nearly broke into coarse guffaws—which would, of course, have blown everything.

Athena was laid out in the family cemetery alongside Roy and not far from the little annex where the Fish animals had been buried over the years. This annex was crowded with small markers dating back to the early 1920's and included countless dogs, an ostrich, several swine, and a kangaroo, upon whose marker was carved:

Rosalee
A Kangaroo
Born: ? Died: 14 August 1937
The Heart of Lovingkind Will Understand

Much furniture was cleared out and replaced with new pieces more to Pearl's liking—Ernie didn't care, he made clear: whatever Pearl liked was fine with him, saluting her with his snifter from the head of the stairs and turning to his chamber, which had been Roy Fish's, years ago: a grand suite overlooking the grounds behind Rounsmeer. Ernie lay on his bed and through his open window gazed across the spacious park, at the neat hedges and sleek, ellipsoidal poplars. . . And waiting, he was rewarded when a peacock sauntered by, its long tail bobbing, lilting, with each slow step, and then fanning its wide, resplendent panoply of eyes. And on occasion, but rarely, Ernie's patience, his yearning, was blessed by a glimpse of Gigi hopping through the park. When she was gone, Ernie sat there, staring once again at hedges and trees, perfect and precise like toys, and through his stupor, in the static amber light, he heard a gardener's shears, the soft, dulcet snipping suspended in the air like the pat of lips.

Ernie made friends with the gardeners and the rest of the staff—quite good friends, in fact, when it was discovered that he had worked with one of them, Jenkins, in the good old days when Cheney held the Jaguar franchise. Pearl caught on quickly to Ernie's new mood, and it inspired her in a way which didn't altogether please Ernie, for now she sketched and photographed the staff so relentlessly they could hardly get their work done, and furthermore, it seemed she didn't have any intentions of ever leaving Rounsmeer for the city.

One evening Pearl came to Ernie's room. She entered without his knowing, and stood watching as he weaved across the room from his decanter on the mantle to the window where he leaned his brow against the window pane, looking across the grounds as he did perhaps a hundred times a day. "Poor Ernie," Pearl said.

"Whoaa. . .!" he bellowed, totally startled, nearly lunging through the window.

She rushed to his side and helped him to a couch. "There, there," she soothed. "This grief you feel for Athena is uncanny. It is *so* much like the grief Roy showed when one of his animals died. And in this very room. . ."

"Nothing. Grief. Mere grief. Some brandy"—for he had dropped his glass.

She leaped to her feet and dashed across the room. Returning with the decanter, she poured some brandy which Ernie downed. "Ahhh," he gasped.

"Perhaps we should go to the city for a while," Pearl said.

He was shaking his head in despair before she finished.

"But you need the company of . . . of the *living,* Ernie love."

"Time's the only healer. Time . . . and solitude."

"Oh no, Ernie love, not solitude."

He nodded his head slowly, painfully. "For me it is. You know, my dear, I am different." He meant his ovalness.

"Yes, Ernie love, and bless you for being different. But I fear that if I leave you here alone. . ."

He shook his head slowly, bravely. "I won't be alone. The staff. Jenkins, Lloyd, and the others."

"Well. If you think it's best," and he was surprised at how quickly she was won over. But it *had* been boring for her out here these two months, photographing the staff and the shrubs. She must be fully desperate to return to the city.

"You hop into town. . . Er. . ." He coughed harshly. "You run along into town, dear Pearl."

She leaned forward, kissed his brow, and whispered, "And now I'll dash down the hall to my room and put on my gown, the green one, and I'll return to you, my true love."

Patting her shoulder, he nodded with his eyes shut, gritting his teeth.

The next morning a festive air prevailed amid a great hubbub of activity—the servants scurried about, making ready for Mrs. Seervus's departure, while Ernie helped a great deal, working right alongside Jenkins and Lloyd, and for a while it was just like old times: Ernie felt the soft, pleasant ache of nostalgia for the days back at Cheney's, and for a moment he even yearned for the rainy days on Houpton Road.

Pearl was finally packed and loaded into the limousine. Jenkins would drive her into the city. The whole staff was out front to see her off. She wept—this was the first time she and Ernie would be apart. "But of course we'll phone," Ernie reminded her, patting her arm. "Oh, but I'll miss you so much," she wept. "There, there, dear Pearl. Be brave," and he winked Jenkins the signal. The large black car pulled slowly away and headed down the driveway, creeping along, following a peacock which finally deigned to move aside and let them pass. Pearl was waving out the round rear window, and as the car passed through the gate, she continued waving, though her face was now invisible to Ernie . . . and then Gigi appeared out of the bushes, looking after the car.

Ernie's heart stopped. He was certain Pearl would see Gigi and suddenly, in a miraculous, horrible flash of understanding, she would realize what was about to happen. Pearl would, just by looking at Gigi's plaintive face, at those large almond eyes, understand everything. The car would halt, slowly turn around, and come back. . .

But the car crept through the gates. The gates swung closed with majestic slowness.

And as Ernie stood on the steps of his mansion, Gigi turned, and even from a hundred yards Ernie saw those deep, meaningful eyes and knew what was in them.

Ernie, Jenkins, and Lloyd were talking on the back steps. The tempo was quite different when Mrs. Seervus wasn't around. And Ernie let it be known that he didn't mind. Most of the staff returned to their cottages down the hill in Snell—including, especially, Mrs. Starm, Mrs. Shey, and Miss Gurnen—which left the only woman on the premises the ancient Mrs. Manion whose husband was officially the head of the staff, though he was nearly blind, usually bedridden, and periodically so sorely drunk that he kept both himself and Mrs. Manion out of commission, while she struggled to keep him alive through his routs.

Ernie was explaining to Jenkins and Lloyd how one trains kangaroo. "You see, it's not at all like with bird dogs. Never chastise kangaroo. Very sensitive creatures. You can tell by their eyes."

"D'ye recall Becky?" Lloyd interrupted, asking Jenkins. Becky, they explained, was a pig who lived here years ago. Becky, too, had sensitive eyes. And she was very tidy, too. Liked her bath.

"But of course you can't train pig," Ernie insisted.

"Ye can, but who's interested in pigs?"

Ernie didn't like the sound of that. But he nodded to the essential idea in it. "Right. With kangaroo there's much more that's of interest, you see. People are *interested* in kangaroo. For one thing, not everyone has a kangaroo."

"What can they be trained to do?" Jenkins asked.

"Why, you name it! My Uncle Bob trained his Edith to drink tea, smoke cigarettes, sleep in a bed . . . and perform all kinds of general entertainment tricks such as leaping over obstacles, juggling, costuming. . ."

"Would it wear costumes?"

"Of course. The neatest garbs you could imagine. And the people paid to see her, too. That's the action, you see. Word gets around you've kangaroo dressing up and performing tricks, and you've got something people will appreciate."

"So it's your plan to train Madam Athena's Gigi," Jenkins said.

"Well. . . I hadn't really thought of it that way, Jenkins. But now that you mention it, perhaps it wouldn't be such a *bad* idea."

And within the hour Ernie, Jenkins, and Lloyd were busy converting Pearl's studio into a training arena. This was important. "From now on," Ernie told them that evening when the finishing touches were made, "this will be called the *arena.* Kangaroo are very brilliant creatures. They know what you're saying about them most of the time. So if we're . . . if *I'm* going to train her, she must know from *all* of us that she's a performer, you see. When she's within earshot, which will be most of the time, because kangaroo have the keenest hearing of all creatures, you must remember to speak of her in a highly respectful manner and keep in mind that she is a *performer.* Now. Any questions?"

There were none.

"Tomorrow it begins," he said, and he trembled from head to foot.

The next morning after breakfast, Ernie climbed into the gardeners' electric cart and went looking for Gigi. First, down to the pond. Then along the bushes that concealed the rock ledge behind the pond. Her tracks were everywhere, but he couldn't find her. Next, Ernie hummed along in the little cart behind the garage and up the long park that crested at a sheer rock cliff overlooking a stream, far below, the rolling hills of the countryside, and in the distance the small village of Snell. A gazebo was atop the hill, set safely back from the cliff, and it was there Ernie found Gigi.

She sat on a wooden bench, and on the table before her she had spread the fistfuls of flowers she had stolen from the garden and which she was now slowly eating while she stared off across the distance.

She glanced at Ernie as he switched off the electric cart and approached the gazebo, but then she looked back to her vista and continued nibbling the flowers. He stepped into the gazebo and sat across the table from her. Her large deep eyes shifted to his, then down at the flowers before her. With her nimble paws, tipped by long black claws, she picked up a rose blossom. Plucking the petals one by one without looking down, she put them to her lips, the pink tip of her tongue flicking out for each petal.

Ernie sat entranced as Gigi ate all the flowers and wiped her mouth. He waited for what she would do next. But she simply sat there, her forelegs hanging down straight over her belly. She stared across the distance, her eyes only glancing at Ernie now and then, as if to see if he were still there.

Slowly Ernie rose. He moved to the side of the table. Farther. Slowly. He reached out. . .

He touched her shoulder. It was sleek, the fur even softer than he had imagined. He stroked her. He moved nearer and put his arm around her shoulders. His heart pounding so hard he was certain it would burst, he stood there, tears streaming down his face.

When he regained control, he looked at her.

But she still stared off—perhaps at the village below.

A wind moved up the cliff and burst over its top, catching some flower stems on the table and scattering them. After the breeze had passed, a strange coldness remained—a coldness as tangible to Ernie as if it were a third person in the gazebo. And then Ernie realized the coldness hadn't come with the wind; it originated in Gigi.

"I. . ." he said out loud, but couldn't finish. He mutely stood there, his arm around her shoulders, until Gigi moved away, gently but firmly. She hopped out of the gazebo and turning homewards, headed down the hill, quickly picking up speed, soon covering fifteen feet with each bound.

The training wasn't only for the sake of Jenkins and the others—Ernie knew word would soon reach the village that the gentleman at Rounsmeer was training the late Athena Fish's kangaroo to perform tricks. But the training was undertaken for Ernie's sake as well. And for Gigi's sake, too. Ernie felt the honest need to . . . *do* something; he was obliged to make a worthy contribution. Which roughly were the sentiments and guiding principles of his Uncle Bob—what Ernie could recall of them. Time and again he tried to draw from memory Bob's ramblings concerning duty, showmanship, and kangaroo. But nearly all of it was lost except indistinct echoes that seemed to return only in the bleary gray hours of dawn.

Gigi learned fairly well. But there was still that reticence, and it was ruining Ernie. Perhaps Gigi was simply cold. It was possible. Or perhaps she had a polite but definite dislike of Ernie. He tried a different cologne. A dozen different colognes. *No* cologne. But it made no difference. He changed his wardrobe—but she was indifferent to him no matter what he wore. Then it stuck him that she was grieving the passing of Athena Fish. This possibility gave Ernie new hope; for if it was grief, the mood was bound to pass. Eventually. But how long would it take?

Then the horrible thought lodged in his mind that Gigi's outlook was characteristically kangaroo. He recalled those evenings with Bob and Edith—Edith across the table silently sipping tea while Bob talked, while Ernie watched Edith's every move. That essential mystery in Edith, which had so firmly and fatally attracted Ernie, could have been this very same wistfulness Ernie encountered in Gigi. And no doubt it had been Edith's reticence that destroyed Bob. At the time of his visits to them, Ernie had been too young to understand. But *Bob* knew. Oh yes! And that was why Bob had driven himself—and Edith—so relentlessly those last years. So relentlessly, so fiercely that Edith broke under the great pressure of Bob's attempts to . . . *possess* her. Edith killed Bob rather than surrender.

Ernie sobbed aloud, knowing what special hell it is to love kangaroo.

When Pearl returned to Rounsmeer she wasn't altogether pleased to find her studio converted into a training area, littered with large balls, hoops, and gaudy silk costumes which Ernie had the good Mrs. Manion sewing both night and day.

But Pearl was intrigued with the idea of Ernie's project. Ernie seemed to have recovered from his grief over the death of Athena. But he hadn't completely returned to himself—and Pearl confronted him with it one evening.

She told him she felt he was rather distant—though his spirits seemed quite high. Ernie didn't reply, but peered at her over the rim of his snifter. Pearl sighed, expressed rather vaguely that she was pleased that he was at least *some* better, and the next day she returned to the city, promising she would be back just as soon as she could—though her latest project would take her to Gibraltar for two weeks.

Two weeks!

Time, Ernie cried within himself, was the answer! Time would do it, and when Pearl departed, Ernie's heart filled with anticipation and delight as he bounded into the electric cart and urged it up the hill to the gazebo where he found Gigi, staring off into the distance.

They had spent most of the day working with the bicycle. Jenkins had mounted Mr. Manion's decrepit two-wheeler with a motorcycle's banana seat, bolted large wooden slats to the pedals, and bound elevated handlebars with heavy twine for a good grip—Gigi was slowly learning the bike. Wearing a pink singlet and a white tutu, she could manage the bike on her own for nearly six feet before she started leaning to the side—to be caught by Ernie, trotting along behind. But Gigi's heart wasn't in it, Ernie could tell. She would have been much happier in the gazebo. But Ernie was by now madly dedicated to teaching her to ride. Feverishly he drove himself and Gigi. Ten, twelve hours a day. And when his hand brushed against her, he hardly noticed.

On that particular day Ernie had worked with Gigi on the bicycle since early morning, not stopping for lunch except to hand her a cookie from the lunch tray Mrs. Manion brought to the training arena.

Trotting behind Gigi as she rode slowly along, her hindlegs slowly revolving with the pedals, her smooth neck arched in concentration as she looked down at the front wheel. . . *That* was why she couldn't ride! *She looked down*!

"Look *up*. Look *up,*" Ernie bellowed. "Look where you're going, you stupid brute. The front wheel's doing all right. Don't worry about it. Look up. Look up."

And Gigi wobbled worse, tilted hazardously to the side, and this time Ernie didn't catch her but let her crash to the floor.

"Oh bleeding Jesus," Ernie shouted at the ceiling. He looked down at her, tangled in the foolish bike, her ears down, the tip of her tail stuck through the spokes, and Ernie shook his fist at her. "I ought to just let you lie there, you lummox." And as he stared down at her, their eyes locked, he heard, for the first time, the sound of kangaroo: a deep, woeful moan unlike any sound Ernie had every heard. It stole the breath from him. His mouth hanging open, staring into Gigi's eyes, Ernie suddenly understood that when he had encountered her at the gazebo that afternoon, so long ago it seemed, he had rushed at her with awful impatience—*brutal* impatience. And then, repulsed by her delicacy, he had tried to break her will in the training arena—he had been doggedly trying to bring her around, snap her out of it. And all the while she had been silently, with the patience of beasts, drawing him to her. "Oh my," he said softly in a tone quite similar to the moan that Gigi had uttered, and Ernie flung the wretched bicycle aside: their love, their simple, everlasting bond as creatures, was consummated.

He lived in a room with a narrow window looking north on Houpton Road. The first week of each month, his settlement check in hand, he trudged to the pub. The last three weeks he sat in his room and waited. When his hand was steady enough, he worked a few hours a day for a greengrocer, a patient man who knew that by and by this one would tell his story, just as all the others had.

The greengrocer's hands sorted through the rutabagas and turnips with the firm gentleness of a nursemaid's, and again and again he showed Ernie how to trim the vegetables, but it seemed he couldn't learn. Once, when they were working with Brussels sprouts, Ernie broke his silence to remark that this had been his Gigi's favorite dish–Brussels sprouts with cheese sauce. The greengrocer smiled kindly and said to himself, "Here it comes."

Telling his wife the story later, the greengrocer decided Ernie's story wasn't so awfully different from those of other boozers whose losing their true love had ruined them for looking into all the faces that one must if he is to live out his time in a normal way. And the ending of the story seemed especially trite to the greengrocer, though his wife didn't agree. But of course she hadn't heard all the stories her husband had–he only told her the best.

For weeks, months, maybe even a year or two, Ernie and Gigi were alone, nearly, at Rounsmeer: Ernie sent the household staff permanently down the hill to Snell, all but old Mrs. Manion who, after the death of her husband, lost concern for this life in her growing interest in the next. So Ernie and Gigi's time glowed in private, pristine winter afternoons, mellow and amber, by the fire, sipping tea and gazing into the flames where a thousand fantastic cities were born and consumed, while outside the poplars moaned in the wind, swayed their naked arms against the sky.

Then Pearl appeared, returning unexpectedly from the city ("This part is common," the greengrocer told his wife.) Pearl shouted, stamped, and shook her fist at Ernie—while Gigi nimbly ducked out the door and went hopping down the hall—Thank God, Ernie sighed. Pearl, her eyes bulged into large ovals, picked up a marble statue and closed in on Ernie for the kill. He broke. With Pearl chasing him, Ernie lumbered down the front stairs, up the back, through the halls, down again, out the front door, over the grounds, even to the gate—but Pearl had locked it: there was no escape. She caught him the first time when he was again in the house. She choked him, threw him down the stairs, and hammered him nearly senseless with a broken chair leg.

This went on for days. At night, when the fighting let up, Ernie drank himself unconscious, hiding in one of the small rooms in the servants' quarters. Early one morning he went looking for Gigi, but couldn't fine her—and he was thankful, for if he couldn't find her, neither could Pearl.

And then came the crisis. Exhausted, without hope, it was time for Ernie to perish or relent.

Telling the greengrocer, Ernie said simply, "I relented," but the word was heavy with grief.

It happened one morning when they were fighting before breakfast—though Mrs. Manion's biscuits and soft-boiled eggs would only have been used as missiles. The fighting that morning raged all through the first floor, up the stairs, and then they tumbled all the way downstairs. Ernie relented at the foot of the stairs: he grabbed Pearl's leg, tripping her, and, to keep her from springing to her feet, he vigorously bounced himself on top of her. The passion of the fight was magically transformed.

When they were done, and looked at each other in the calm way man and wife will, Ernie happened to glance at a window. There he saw the narrow face, the slender neck and shoulders.

Immediately she disappeared from the window. She bounded through the park and up the hill toward her gazebo, with Ernie, half dressed, chasing after her, followed by Pearl.

Ernie reached the top of the hill. There Gigi perched on the edge of the cliff, staring off, as ever, as if searching the distance for her native land, or searching for that life which is beyond even the keen vision of kangaroos. In that long moment Ernie realized he could never have Gigi—*all* of her. And he knew, finally, the complete despair his Uncle Bob felt, the futility—the loss an old lover feels when he gazes for the last time into the death glazed eyes.

Gigi glanced over her shoulder at Ernie. Without a sound, she flexed her mighty hind legs and leaped. She plummeted farther than distance and time. She glided into the gray air of memory, into Ernie's soul, where she would live in the loneliness and mystery that are love.

A NORTHERN MEMOIR

They would arrive at dusk so the large rental truck could pass unnoticed down our main street and through the campus. Professor Czoc would be driving; her husband would ride in back with the books and things. She would soon find the road out to the old Wervel place, and when they topped the hill overlooking us all, Professor Czoc would masterfully back the truck through the stone gate, up the winding drive and across the lawn, weaving deftly through the bushes and trees without crunching a shrub or snapping a branch, to butt the truck just short of the same French doors which I see from my office. I just might have been standing at my window that night observing in a sense the Czoc's arrival, though I would have seen only my own dark reflection. In the following weeks how often I gazed up at that large house, where shadows roamed like mournful clouds behind the windows and French doors.

We met our new colleague at a party welcoming her and commemorating, at least for some, the retirement of Chuff Freyme. Poor Chuff had let himself be lured into a labyrinth from which there was no hope of ever finding his way—not that he wanted out after he came eye to eye with the great sleek thing which lurks in the center of labyrinths.

Lothar and I had just arrived at the party and were taking off our coats when Chuff, purple-pale, rushed up and with the mawkish earnestness of drunks, said, "I should have worn disguises. I should never have been where I was believed to be."

Lothar put his hand on Chuff's shoulder, his thumb in the divot of his collar bone, and moved him. For he was blocking Lothar's view of Professor Czoc across the room, tall and elegant in a metallic green gown.

I led Chuff aside and heard him out, and, poor soul, though his realizations and insights were rather late, he was right: long ago he ought to have planned on always being elsewhere, and as often as humanly possible he should have been someone else. Instead, he had held his breath, crossed his fingers, and prayed he wouldn't get caught so long as he didn't let loose in wide extravaganzas but limited himself to brisk, spontaneous stunts. But the accummulation of pecadillos eventually went rumbling out from under Chuff like a thousand lumpy little potato heads, trophies of his gnome-hunts in the labyrinth. So predictable was his downfall that his "retirement" fluttered gossips for only a week.

"There, there," I said and patted his arm. He smiled wanly, enjoying this.

Tonight's party would console him. And tomorrow, hungover, Chuff would load his things off to Moon Lake. He would read, reflect, and perhaps some afternoon take up again his brushes and palette, and thus plunge into the lonely dawdling that waits a lifetime for us. When he let himself, he would stare off, recollecting Dipsweth's dim, narrow-windowed classrooms, the chalk dust, the aroma of students, while out the cabin window Fall's abject beauty would slip forgetfully to duller, formidable hues, and further, with the customary inevitability of things, to the burials of winter.

Professor Czoc turned without expression when Lothar spoke to her. She went into another room, stood outside a group, and soon became its center, though she seldom spoke and obviously wasn't listening to the prattle. (Perhaps she listened for a far off sound: Was Czoc, alone tonight on Wervel Hill, calling to her?)

Lothar stood back as others offered themselves to Professor Coc in that dauntless, puppetlike way men do. They flashed their teeth and laughed for her. Standing on tiptoes they took a good look right into her, and—my! they liked what they saw. One could distinctly hear the idea plink in each of them, and in their wives, too, whose hearts in creamy breasts surged up with hatred and adoration: "Why, she's . . . beautiful!"

The phonograph blared. We hopped and frisked, the floor flexing under us, and because Professor Czoc would not dance, it appeared we were dancing for her. Later there was scuffling and hilarity, and in the Game Room we threw darts at each other. Then food was spread and we feasted, braying in each others' faces; the steaming meat and our breath clouded our spectacles.

Afterwards I found poor Chuff, riddled with darts, crumpled in a corner. I nudged him with my toe and as he rolled over he mumbled, "Farewell." (He is already out at Moon Lake, wobbling through a fantasy with Professor Czoc: they stroll through the woods and Chuff explains himself, the pique and joy. We're amused, gazing across the lake into his dream: Professor Czoc is much taller than our anemic Chuff, and several times we see her grinning exaggeratedly over his head and laughing silently. And we're further amused when, widening focus, we see others watching: behind every tree and bush someone hides–a friend here, an enemy there.)

Lothar reached down and jerked Chuff upright. With his hands under Chuff's armpits and with Chuff's feet on top his, Lothar marched him into the bathroom. As I pushed the door shut after them, Lothar was bending Chuff over the sink.

I crossed the room to where Professor Czoc listened icily to a young instructor in the art department named D. H. Lawrence, who had grown a beard and dyed it red. Discoursing at length, putting on quite a show for Professor Czoc, he sliced and boxed the air with both hands. He ached to paint her: a reclining nude which he would shatter into a thousand shards and then, flinging aside his paints and pants, lunge onto her. . .

Coming from the bathroom, Lothar crept up behind Professor Czoc. He stared over her shoulder at D. H. Lawrence, who tried to continue but faltered. "All right. What do you want?" Lawrence said.

Professor Czoc thought this was meant for her, and her eyes tightened.

Lothar put his face in Professor Czoc's hair and whispered in her ear.

She spun about, backing from him as he opened his mouth wide.

"I have nothing to say to you," Professor Czoc said.

"You've answered my question." He motioned for D. H. Lawrence to be off. Frowning, the young man obeyed.

Lothar quickly stepped in front of Professor Czoc and backed her to the wall. He unbuttoned his jacket and revealed a blood red vest with gold buttons.

Professor Czoc glanced at the vest, down the row of buttons, then up to his eyes. She stared flatly at him. And then she smiled–archly, boldly. In her eyes there was defiance and expectancy. Was she aware this was the same smile she would give across a bed as she lifted her arms to unclasp her hair? Lothar made a great business of licking his lips, his tongue lolling far out.

"Disgusting!" Professor Czoc said. She looked at me as if I were to blame. "This man has tormented me all evening."

I smiled. "He follows his course with the precision and security of a sleepwalker."

"What?" she said. "What's that. . .?"

But Lothar leaned forward and said, "Wanda, I've got you now. And I know about Czoc, too."

I whispered, "A secret?" She glanced at me. "You and your husband will find tremendous seclusion. The endless snows, the impassable roads, the great woods and winding paths."

"Simply because my husband couldn't come. . ."

"There's Moon Lake, famous for its steep banks and leaden depths."

Lothar said, "You've made a mistake with Czoc. He's not for you."

"How exasperating," she said. But her eyes were fading to vacant pathos as if right there before us she had begun dreaming. She leaned against the wall and spoke barely above a whisper, "Who are you?"

I stepped nearer. "This Northern land is Lothar's ancestral home, to which he returned last month for old time's sake. He previously held tenure at a renown institution not unlike Dipsweth." I ran my hand up her smooth arm. "And could it be your Czoc, too, is returning to the breeding grounds?"

At that moment Chuff Freyme came up and said in Lothar's face, "Treacherous jerk!"

Lothar spun Chuff about and, gripping his shoulders, held him straight. "Look. How do you like it, Wanda?"

Lothar turned him around and said, "All right, Freyme, play dead."

Professor Czoc slid to the side and out the door.

Lothar would have followed, but Chuff grabbed his lapels and with his face in Lothar's, his purple lips puckering, said, "You're killing me. You know that, don't you? Don't you?"

"Ha!" Lothar shot his hands between Chuff's, breaking his grip. He shoved Chuff and bounding from the room reached the door at the same time Chuff crashed into a china closet.

Lothar ran from room to room but it wasn't until he looked out a small round window on the staircase that he saw a car pulling off—the same car I would often see from my office window descending Wervel Hill.

Lothar returned, his eyes big, amazed. We stepped into a dark room and he bucked in my arms as he sobbed.

On one of those crisp Saturday mornings when men in our town don old duds and rake leaves, or saw wood and smiling, cap in hand, surprise widows on their back porches, I drove up Wervel Hill.

The old two-story house, inhabited for years by the Wervels, who had enjoyed success in several enterprises, would now have the icy brightness of Professor Czoc's touch: green and white would slide smoothly into each other, the rooms a-prance with wee gazelles, blue glass griffins, wings spread and rearing into flight through ivy. Professor Czoc, the mysterious Czoc, and I, would sit in a sunny room. Professor Czoc would wear a flowing peignoir, mauve, or darker, her hair loose, allowing sensitive nostrils to catch the cheesy complacency of sleep. Our conversation would be beautifully tedious, and elaborate exercise in restraint, interminable. By and by, Czoc would step from the room to fetch his pipe or look out the study window at the feeder, where he feared a huge white cat was molesting the birds. I would then, speaking low, come to the point. Professor Czoc would lean forward, touching the table with the tips of her fingers. She would rise and rather wistfully leave me sitting in the sun-bright room amid zinnias and white curtains. . . Czoc, dottering fool, blind in one eye and milky in the other, would return, apologizing befuddledly, at which he would be a master, having recently retired from a career of fatuity. He wed his wife by grand fluke; she stays with him because she is, alas, easily controlled: he caned her once, or at the beginning he subdued her with a Great Dane. . .

I reached the end of the winding driveway. When I knocked at the door, the echo sank into the house. I walked around the side. Brown curtains dense as earth covered the windows. As I stepped onto the terrace above the garden, the curtains weren't shut, and I caught a glimpse not of a sunroom with droll ivy and boisterous zinnias.

I looked into nothing. A room so enormous the far wall was hidden by the day's reflection on the glass. No furniture or new-painted walls with pictures, no glass tables with bowls of fruit. No flurry of peignoir with a surprised, trilling, "Eek!"

The entire first floor was a cavern, the walls knocked out, the huge house beams exposed. Framing my face to the window, I saw laboratory apparatus sprouting on work benches, an arbor of copper glass tubes hiding small black boxes. Beyond the branches lay a great shadow like a pile of broken sofas.

Then the brown curtain crushed my view, the pulley beyond the pane screaming derisively, yet forlornly.

Several days later I stood before the science building, a monstrosity of three old buildings interconnected: an ancient, crooked dormitory; Dipsweth's original administration building; and what had once been a railway round-house.

When I entered, the building at first seemed deserted. But deep within, where the odors of gases, old fruit, and wet fur, hung in the air, specialists scurried along, staying close to the walls and darting into offices niched in the corners of the twisting corridors. These runty, yellowish individuals were involved in the research for which Dipsweth was well known; they were Asiatics, Lapps, and Pygmy scholars who from years in the lab were bleached a pasty ochre.

I found Professor Czoc's office hidden on the fourth floor. The door was ajar and the tiny room was filled with a jumble of crates, books, and filing cabinets. At the end of a trail through all this, a white telescope stood before a window no wider than a slit but providing a view of the house on Wervel Hill and the woods beyond.

The hulking shadows stirred in the office and I heard whispering. I pushed the door open wider and saw a desk where Professor Czoc sat with none other than Dipsweth's star athelete, Buck O'Brian, a neckless, huge-shouldered lad who, a veteran of perhaps too many seasons, had been so thoroughly socked about that his features had solidified to perpetual bovine woe. (Returning from a walk in the woods early one morning, I passed a field at the edge of town where a crowd of men were fighting. I watched from behind a tree and realized they were ruggers playing by Dipsweth's rules. Before a row of wooden chairs they beat and stomped each other in silence. At the far end of the field the ball was being trundled off into the woods by a squat, dark creature, perhaps a badger.)

Apparently Buck O'Brian had excellent hearing, though his ears resembled snails nailed to his head; he looked over his shoulder at me. His brows were thickly plastered and beneath them his face was a suave blend of black and purple.

"Professor Czoc is expecting me," I said from the doorway.

"I was not expecting you," said Professor Czoc, pushing her swivel chair from the desk and slowly crossing her legs. "What do you want?"

"My business is of a highly personal nature," I said.

She touched Buck O'Brian's forearm with two fingertips and the young man rose. I hurried right up and sat in his chair. He stepped out of the office, turned, and lifting his arms, leaned against the doorframe as if he might push the door apart and bring the building down on us.

I began. "Coming from the world at large to Dipsweth and our shrouded village, you will have several difficulties grasping situations. There has been early shame, and, all in all, no little travail. But surprising coups have set things straight, and we live it down, somehow, deriving solace from the quietude so oppressive to newcomers and outsiders." I sighed. "You've no idea what we're really doing here."

"Oh, I think I have a notion," Professor Czoc said, her eyes bright as dimes.

"I suppose you mean that, as a lady of science, you're up on Dipsweth's recent history—the experiments of the 1940's, the great Biblical beast scandal, and that laughable conference on angels where Jung made a fool of himself.

"I congratulate you on your scientific accomplishments, on your astonishing beauty, and your popularity with one and all. . ." The doorframe cracked loudly. "However, there is more to Dipsweth than science. Perhaps you have two or three facts, which you've stuffed up a pants leg and made a scarecrow. You've read dreams and even dreamed on your own. You've kept your ears open for every deranged rumor, and you've no doubt spun a legend or two yourself during summer vacations and published them in the Fall as contributions to the field. . ."

Professor Czoc interrupted. "Come to the point. You're afraid of losing that . . . person of yours, aren't you? That great buffoon what's-his-name."

"No, there's plenty of Lothar for everyone. But Lothar *is* the reason you've come here, though you don't truly grasp it yet.

"Lothar knew the moment he saw you. And it was a great anthropologic moment—historic, though ultimately in that category of anthropology reserved for feats of horror. But how could you connect Lothar with legends and vague rumor?"

"Please," Professor Czoc said, holding up a hand. "I have no idea what this is all about, but rest assured I'm not here for your Lothar.

Science has brought me to Dipsweth, not your legends or your breeding grounds."

I looked away and after a moment said in my calmest manner, "Though you have no idea, bless your pretty skin, what the breeding grounds are and what transpires, you have indeed come to them. And now you must leave. This instant!"

She leaned back and said, "Leave? Why, I'm exactly where I want to be, and I know exactly what I want."

"Listen." I lifted my hands and spread my fingers. "You know what you want, but you have no idea how you'll get it." I stared into her intently. She could understand if she would only try. But she wanted more. "Listen."

A triumphant laugh exploded in the corridor. Shoving Buck O'Brian out of the way, Lothar strode into the office. I rose and went to the white telescope as Lothar grinned down at Professor Czoc and said richly,

"Ding dong bell;
Pussy's in the well.
Who put her there?–
Little Dewey Dare.
Who'll get her out?–
Big Dick Stout."

He dragged up a crate and sat on it with his knees touching Professor Czoc's. He said low, "I want to tell you how much I liked our chitchat at the party. I've come to pursue it with my best."

"You again," she said.

He scooted still closer, ramming a knee between hers. He whispered, "Remember what we were saying?"

"As a matter of fact, no."

He unbuttoned his jacket, letting it tent their knees and thighs. Putting his face almost in hers, he said, "I have brought a great treasure."

"I would rather," Professor Czoc said, "hear the legend."

"Which one?"

"There are more than one?"

"Twenty, thirty. There's Happy Joseph. He became a frog. Eight feet long from head to toe when he stretched out on the bank to sun. You want the rest?"

"Yes."

"Ha! Happy Joseph got itchy. Interfered with the girls' gym class at their swimming lessons. So he got hauled away."

"Is he dead, then?"

"Dead?" Lothar laughed with all his might. "Did you say *dead*?"

I looked into the telescope: it was focused on the woods–on Moon Lake. There was Chuff Freyme's cabin, and as I looked, the door flew open and out came Chuff, running like mad. "It looks bad for Chuff Freyme," I said.

"Freyme," Professor Czoc said to Lothar. "Tell me about him."

Grinning, Lothar opened his jaws wide and banged them shut. As he spoke he wagged his leg between her knees, swiveling her slowly back and forth. "He was searching for his big dream ideal. And when he got it, they fired him. Ha!"

She closed her eyes, leaning back as if dizzy from the swaying.

"Something's after Chuff!" I said.

Lothar got up and, pushing me aside, looked into the telescope. "Hm. Freyme's in for it good this time."

Lothar walked back to the desk and tilting back Professor Czoc's chair, wedged open her knees. Buck O'Brian slowly came and stood beside him.

Tiptoeing up the path between the crates, I glanced back. Shoulder to shoulder, they leaned over her. Buck O'Brian reached down; either he lifted one of her legs, or she lifted it at his touch. As I shut the door, Lothar turned the telescope to perhaps give Professor Czoc a wrong-way look at Chuff Freyme and his tormentor, or perhaps Lothar, his face serene in concentration, his arms extended from his sides as he leaned over the instrument, was expressing a sudden interest in science and would peer down the telescope into Professor Czoc.

At dawn I go to Moon Lake: a bumblebee in hardening paraffin, I move with incredible slowness. As if wandering off as people sometimes do, I pass through the high-hedged lane, and finding by dull magic my car I drive under the low sky through the woods and take the Moon Lake turn-off. Clumps of snow hide bushes, shroud evergreens, pack the crotches of trees. The road lobs off where stuck cars in struggling to free themselves dug great holes. I round a curve and see Moon Lake, a flat lead face staring at the sky. Above it the cabin leans back on itself. On the porch I call, "Chuff? Oh Chuff!" I open the door, call again. I go to the end of the porch, then behind the cabin. Up the hill I see a man, dark as leather, shirtless and barefoot, upside-down in the trees, his stick-man arms straight down, one leg straight up and the other gone at the knee. My heart thrums in my ears. Through the black branches I stare at the rope tied to the ankle. The leg points accusingly at the rope and at the tree limb. I run slowly up the hill and stop, my breath steaming, eye to tiny eye with the face ballooned with the whole body's blood which gravity called to earth, the blood answering as far as it could come. I go down to my car and carefully turn it around. I drive slowly and stopping several times I have only to stare into the woods a few moments before hanging men, some stretched in X's between trees, emerge through the dense branches. In town they hang along telephone lines. One dangles by his wrist from a flagpole. Driving through the campus, I see a fringe of them along the eaves of the science building. I proceed up Wervel Hill, and of course no one answers when I knock. But this time when I turn the corner of the house I find Professor Czoc standing in the garden with a giant.

Mr. Czoc wore a coat of gray tarpaulins sewn together; the one covering most of his back said *Wervel Oldsmobile–Rocket 88.* On his head he wore a flesh-colored shower cap.

Professor Czoc was speaking intently, though the giant appeared not to listen, his heavy-lidded eyes downcast, his mouth sagging on a chin big as a shoe. Then his face flashed with a smile which vanished immediately–a tic that yanked up, then dropped, half his face. Professor Czoc leaned back and said up to him: "And fire." Or perhaps it was "Unfair." The giant shook his head and moaned.

They heard me on the gravel path and turned. "At last I have the pleasure," I said, going forward. Professor Czoc looked away, and Czoc closed his eyes as I seized his hand. "Allow me to welcome you home."

Czoc pulled his hand free and started toward the house. Professor Czoc followed, and walking close to her I said low, "I see Lothar was right about your husband. He remembered the large Czocs who lived here a hundred years ago. But tell me, has it done any good, bringing Czoc back?"

On hands and knees Czoc crawled through the French doors. We walked through behind him, and as he crawled to the far end of the room, I went to a telescope standing before a window and through it looked down at the village. "I have rather important news."

Did I detect a certain urgency in her voice when she said, "I frankly do not. . ."

"It pertains to a certain individual you were involved with the other day."

"I was involved with a number of individuals. Which do you mean?"

"My. I was referring to a rather athletic consultation. . ."

She stepped nearer. "Buck O'Brian?" she said low.

I chuckled. "Hardly. I meant the real thing." Through the telescope I spotted Lothar running down a street. He cut through a yard and burst into a house. Men, women, and children flew from the house, some leaping from windows. Lothar, his mouth wide, came running out, chasing first this one, then another. He stood in the yard, his breath making a cloud. Then he spun about, dived into some shrubberies, and dragged out a man by the leg.

I turned from the telescope. "Now that I've met Czoc I see just how really interested you are in the real thing. I suppose you brought him here hoping he would . . . revive. But he hasn't, has he?" She very slowly closed her eyes as if she would dream away from my words. "No, of course not," I said, "for Czoc is only a giant, a big dud."

I swung the telescope around and looking at her through the big end, saw her miles away, tiny but distinct. "Now for the important news. You came to Dipsweth on a quest. I am pleased to announce the goal of that quest is at hand. You'll soon be getting it. Lift your arms. To unclasp your hair. Now—that smile. . ."

"Ha!" Lothar trotted through the French doors. He heaved a work bench out of his way, smashing the machines and glass tubing; through the telescope the shattering glass flew like a slow cascade of stars.

He grabbed her hair and jerked back her head. While he licked her face, he ripped off her skirt and slip. He bowed her backwards and with his free hand grabbed her. "Pudding!" He released her, gave her a whack, and sent her running for the stairs. He squinted at her as she ran upstairs, and turning to Czoc and me, said, "That's one sweet slice of gick." He charged up the stairs. "Slick gick! Tapioca pudding!"

Czoc grumbled at the far end of the room. I walked down to him. "Quite right, old fellow," I said. "But try to bear up. It's nearly finished. Listen." In the distance dogs were howling. Czoc cried, and as he did his tic lurched his face into its great grin, which immediately slumped. "There, there," I said and patted his hand.

The first of the hounds came bounding around the corner, their claws clattering, their ears pricked as they stared at Czoc and me for an uncertain moment. "You're warm, lads," I called and waved them toward the stairs. They tore across the room and up the stairs.

We heard cars and trucks coming up the drive. There was a commotion, then thunder crashed through the house as the front door was attacked by axes. Firemen, policemen, and fellows with pitchforks and big sticks, marched through, pale and resolute as they followed the dogs upstairs.

I whispered good-bye to Czoc and slipped out. Following a path into the woods, I went to the top of Wervel Hill and sat on a stump. The banging around in the house was muffled and hollow. Then a profound crash shook the house and all was silent.

They somehow got chains on Lothar, and with one end hooked to the bumper of a flat-bed truck, dragged him out. They chained him onto the truck, and as they started off, Lothar saw me on the hill. He called my name again and again.

I send Czoc off each morning and watch from afar as he moves along the hedge-lined lane through the campus, and much later I see his great shadow gliding across the windows in the laboratory in that part of the science building which was once a roundhouse: he works into the night, while the rest of us lie in bed or slump by our dark lamps.

The former Professor Czoc now and then writes us, but her interests have shifted; she is making headway in artistic areas with the acclaimed painter of shards, D. H. Lawrence.

Last week's letter from Lothar complained of the food and begged me for cigarette money. He claims he is much improved, and this seems true. But the officials assure us he will remain in chains until that institution crumbles—and that the day before that occurs he will be transferred to another and from there to another. . . By then the rest of us will be gone, never to return, and also by then, inevitably, Lothar's records will have turned to dust or will have gotten misplaced. The new officials, unable to explain why Lothar is being held, will in embarrassment and shame give him a parole, or whatever such releases will be called in that distant era. Lothar will have long forgotten us—even, sadly, myself. His thoughts will be on the future.

In a new suit of clothes, rather too small for him, and carrying a cardboard suitcase with a change of socks and shorts, he will head North, not knowing why, yet drawn to a distant village, which by then might well be no more than a clearing in the forest.

AWAY IN NIGHT

He lay listening in the darkness. He knew what woke him, but he didn't let himself think about it. Then he heard the noise again—out back, as if they were trying to get in the barn. Then the noise seemed to slowly swing around the house, and they weren't out by the barn but down where the road bends and heads up toward the house, and in the darkness he could see them smoothly loping up the road, their mouths open, their long red tongues lolling out, their eyes set and narrow, staring through the darkness at him.

It was a dream, that was all. He turned on his side and was nearly asleep again when he heard them out front, their voices half-choked, speaking low among themselves. They wouldn't howl, not yet, with their heads tilted back, eyes nearly closed, their lips strangely puckered as if kissing the moon. The howling would come later . . . And just then their voices broke, gave way to rapid, eager whining, and he realized they were coming nearer. They had come around the bend and now by their petulant dog-like whining he could tell they were down where his old, unused turn-off joined the road.

He lay still, listening, not admitting it but knowing he was waiting and hoping for them to pass his turn-off and go on down the road.

But they didn't. He knew they wouldn't.

Now their voices were louder—not because they were howling but because they were nearer, and he knew they were by now inside his gate, and he saw them sniffing the trunks of the two maple trees . . . Then they started howling.

His heart swelled in him like a bubble and his mouth opened and he moaned in the darkness and it joined their cold full howling which rose blue and black in the darkness, rising with such volume it sent steel through the sky and suddenly everything—the wide flat fields, the sky, even the darkness of night itself—shone a cold and radiant blue.

He stood to the side of the window and, reaching out, slowly closed it. In the front room of the house he swung the door shut and slid the bolt.

Then he went down the short hall, his left hand lifted and guiding him along the worn-smooth paper on the wall. Through the kitchen he went to the back room. "Bob," he whispered. Following the heavy snoring he went to the cot and shook him. Bob woke calmly, not at all surprised or alarmed. "Ella Ud Te," he said, talking in the way no one but the old man could understand—and he could understand it only because he had lived nearly thirty years out here in darkness with the boy.

"Get up," he told Bob. "There's wolves out there."

"Wolves?"

"Big dogs." And as he said this, it struck him that maybe they *were* just dogs—farm dogs out roaming, or, at worst, dogs turned wild. But that howling . . . that was wolves.

"Hear them?" They listened. There was a long clear silence like a broad sheet of metal shining blue under a moon . . . and as the silence stretched on and on he was about to believe that they had gone up the road.

But then a long howl split the silence, a howl strangely deep, almost rumbling, as if groping for speech.

"There." He reached out, found Bob's shoulder, and gripped it hard. "Listen to that."

"Idda woa?" Bob whispered.

"Yes. It's wolves. Come up front and you can see them. They're out by the trees."

They went up through the house, Bob walking heavily, knocking against the rocking chair as he always did when he came into the front room. By the window the old man motioned for Bob to stand back and peek out from the side. "They can see you," he whispered.

"They got good eyes. They can see in the dark like it was daylight. Out there by the trees. See them?"

He waited, knowing Bob was looking.

"Sounds like there's five, ten, maybe more." He waited. "They'll look like dogs, but bigger. Lots bigger. Crissake. There's nothin like a dog about a wolf. See them?"

He heard Bob chomping and swallowing the way he did when he was thinking or taking a good look at something.

"They'll just stay out there a while," the old man said. "Then they'll mosey on. They came down the road. As big as day. Crissake. A pack of wolves come walking *right down the road.* What do you think of that? How many is there? Count them. Like I showed you. One, two . . . "

"One, two . . . "

"And then . . . ?"

"Two . . . "

"*Three.*"

"Three."

The old man straightened up abruptly. "No," he whispered so loudly he was afraid the wolves would hear. "*Tell* me. *You* count. Count the things out there and tell me how many there is."

Bob was silent. In his mind the old man could see Bob standing there by the window blinking his eyes and looking back at him.

"Okay," the old man said. "I'd say there's . . . ten. Yes, ten is about it. Each one of them has a different way of howling. You can tell if you listen close. There's that one with the real deep voice. He's the leader of the pack. And then there's a bunch of smaller voiced ones, them's younger but they're still wolves, damn *sight* they're wolves!"

"What do they do?" Bob asked him.

"They just prowl around. Now that there's towns and cities they got to go at night, so they go at night. And they kill things and eat them."

"They ever kill a man?"

"They do. But more likely it's cattle. They'll kill a calf when they can, and they're bad on pigs, and chickens . . .Christ A'mighty! The *coop*!" He grabbed Bob's shoulder. "Listen. They're going to get the chickens. That's what they're going to do. You hear?"

He knew Bob was nodding his head.

"Say it, boy. You hear?"

"Yes, Uncle Ted."

"Okay. They're going to kill all our chickens and eat them up. And if they do that, we got nothin left. You see?"

"Yes."

"So we got to stop them."

"You and me."

"That's right. So now we've got to stop them. Yessiree. Stop them." He paused and the night was totally silent. He moved nearer the window, turned his head and put his ear to it. "They still out there?"

"Huh?"

"Look out and see if they're still out there."

"No."

"They're not?"

"No."

"You don't see them?"

"I don't see nothin."

"Is there a moon?"

"Huh?"

"Is the moon out?"

"I don't know."

If there wasn't a moon maybe Bob couldn't see them now—especially if they were lying down and starting to move closer to the house . . . Or move *around* the house. That was it. They had got scent of the chickens and while he and Bob had been talking they had slipped around the house to the barn.

"They're after the chickens," he shouted, grabbing for Bob again but missing. "Quick. Out back. Hurry," motioning for Bob to follow, going down the hall again to the kitchen, and then in the kitchen stopping beside the old table, his hand touching the familiar corner. "No." In his mind he saw the barn lit by a huge full moon—the barn and its bare yard glowing in an eerie silver-blue daylight, and he saw wolves, so many he couldn't count them, moving slowly toward the barn. "Don't go out there." He spun around. The house was completely silent. Had Bob already gone out the back door . . . ? "Bob," he shouted. "Don't . . . "

"Huh?"

He was behind the old man.

The old man turned to him. "Don't go out there. If they get into the chickens, that's just that. There's nothin we can do to stop them if they want to get into the chickens. We can't go out there." He found his chair at the table and sat down. He heard Bob sit down at his place.

"There's just nothin we can do. We'll just have to sit in here and listen to them while they kill the chickens."

They sat waiting.

The silence deepened as if the presence of wolves brought forth an even deeper quality of night, an even more tangible silence than that which the old man knew so well. And he knew the wolves weren't after the chickens. No. If they had been after the chickens they wouldn't have stopped there in the front yard, and they wouldn't have howled. Wolves were too smart for that. If they howled in front of your house, you could know they weren't after your chickens.

He got up from the table slowly. "Come with me," he said and heard Bob get up. They went to the front bedroom, to the big closet there. "Dig around in there in all that stuff and see if you can find the shotgun."

"The shotgun?" he said slowly, with dread. Years ago Avery, whose farm was up the road, had shot crows out of his field next to the old man's place. The noise scared Bob and he ran out and hid in the barn.

"Dig it out. We'll have to shoot it to drive them off."

"I don't know where it is."

"It's in there. You look in there and you find it. You hear me?"

"Yes."

"All right. Do it right now. I'm going to stand here and see you do it."

He started looking. The old man heard him scoot the big trunk and knock over a tin can full of buttons and nails.

"I can't find it."

"Keep looking. I got to have it."

Bob looked a little longer and found it. The old man broke it down. Both barrels were empty. "Now get down and look in them cans and jars for shells. They're red and green and they're about this long."

Bob found a shell, then another. The old man loaded the gun and snapped it shut. "*Now* we're ready for them."

Bob went to sleep, his snoring resounding loudly from the kitchen table. The old man sat across the table with the gun across his legs. Several times he woke Bob—the snoring made so much noise he couldn't hear anything. The wolves could have come right up on the back porch and stood on the other side of the door and he wouldn't have heard them. But a minute or two later Bob was asleep again and snoring just as loud as before.

The old man got up and went to the back door and opened it. There was the screen door. It wouldn't stop wolves, but it would slow them down enough for the old man to fire both barrels.

He moved his chair over in front of the screen door and held the gun ready and listened to the night. Now the silence wasn't the eerie, awful silence of before. He heard frogs out at the pond, their steady droning dirge rising and falling in slow waves . . .

He must have dozed, then suddenly he was standing with the gun lifted but not all the way to his shoulder, and though the silence was a wall, he was certain that what woke him was the soft tap of claws as a wolf glided across the porch and into the grass.

He swallowed hard, opened his eyes wide, blinked them against the darkness. Breathing lightly with his mouth open so he could hear better, he waited.

They didn't come up on the porch again, but he knew that now they were trotting around out there. He could hear them, though the sound they made was just beneath hearing. He backed away from the screen door and lifted the gun to his shoulder. He aimed it into the large black well where he knew the doorway was, and waited.

Maybe a wolf was at this moment standing there on the other side of the screen door, not panting, its mouth closed, staring at him with large yellow eyes. Fearless, droll, the wolf faced him until the old man's arms grew weak and he had to lower the shotgun and then, moving very slowly—a sudden movement would startle the wolf and it would come through the screen door—the old man swung the wooden door shut.

So weak he couldn't stand, he lay down right there on the floor and slept, not knowing if he would wake.

Bob didn't want to go because he didn't like Avery and his hired hand. He liked Mrs. Avery fine—she didn't make fun of him, and she always gave him something to eat or something to play with. But she couldn't stop her husband and the hired hand from making fun of Bob and playing jokes on him.

To get Bob to go, the old man told him they were taking money to buy candy from Avery.

Bob led him by one hand, and with the other hand the old man balanced the shotgun on his shoulder—and Bob didn't like that either. The old man didn't mention the wolves. If Bob started thinking about the wolves maybe he would know that if they had been there last night, they could still be around somewhere—like in Avery's woods.

As they walked down the dirt road the old man listened for the wolves and listened for the cold silence that followed the wolves wherever they went. And to keep Bob watching for them, he played a game. He told Bob he could eat pancakes for supper if he saw a red bird before they got to Avery's. He kept reminding Bob to look for red birds, and each time after he reminded him the old man could for a while tell Bob was looking all around.

Then the road passed Avery's woods. The old man felt the cool air that hung in the woods no matter how hot a day it was, and his listening went deep into the heavy silence of the woods. He told Bob to look into the woods for red birds, and when they were past it, the old man took a deep breath, and then Bob shouted, "There's one!"

The old man jerked the gun down from his shoulder, dropped it, fell down in the road looking for it, "The gun. Goddamnit, the gun," he shouted, seeing the wolf running down the road toward them, its eyes narrowed tight, its mouth open, a wolf three, four feet tall, its big head two hands wide, and the old man got the gun and put it to his shoulder, and was on his knees aiming the gun and he shouted, "Where. Where. Tell me. My God, boy, *tell* me," by then knowing it was too late, he could see it leaping, and he clenched his teeth for the impact . . .

"It flew off. You scared it and it went off. Did you want to shoot it?"

The old man stood up. After a moment he put the gun on his shoulder. "Do I get pancakes?" Bob said. They walked on down the road.

Avery and the hired hand were out in the fields. Bob was happy about that. Mrs. Avery had them come in the kitchen and eat pie, and the old man told her about the wolves.

He told her Bob had counted them and there were ten.

"You sure they wasn't just somebody's dogs out slippin around?" Mrs. Avery shouted. She and Avery always yelled at the old man and Bob as if they thought they were hard of hearing.

"They were *wolves,*" the old man said. "Big. Bigger'n any dog. *I* could tell by the way they was howlin. Crissake, it's a warning when you hear a wolf howl."

"Well." The old man could tell she was slipping Bob another piece of pie. That was the way she did—just as soon as Bob would finish one piece, she would put another on his plate, and they didn't think the old man knew what they were up to.

"Where'd you say Avery was?"

"He's back out by Higgs' creek."

"By a creek. That don't sound good to me. They follow water, you know."

"Oh, Avery's all right, Ted. The hired hand's out there, and Tige and old Fuss went out with them. They're good huntin dogs. They wouldn't allow wolves to slip up on Avery."

"Dogs is nothin to a wolf. My God, they just *walk* over dogs."

"Well, I'll tell Avery to keep his eyes open . . . " She cut off short and he heard her picking up the things from the table.

"The candy," Bob said.

"Why you just had *pie*, boy," the old man said.

"What's that he said?" Mrs Avery asked.

"He's just sayin how good the pie was."

"Does he want some more?"

"Oh, no. He's all filled up. And he's havin pancakes tonight for supper, ain't you, boy? He seen him a red bird, so he gets pancakes tonight. That's the way we do things over at our place."

"Well."

The old man and Bob started back up the road and it didn't take nearly as long going back as it had coming.

They fed the chickens and gathered the eggs, and they made sure the coop was shut up tight.

Bob ate his pancakes and went to bed even though the sun was still up—the old man could tell by the birds and the wind.

Along about sundown the old man dozed off sitting in the front room, and when he woke it was still early in the night. He rose to go in to bed and then he heard something out back.

His heart was in his mouth and it was just like last night all over again, he was just as scared, he felt just as sick, even worse, dead-out disappointed and weary. But then he heard the steps on the back porch and knew they were Bob's—he was coming back in from the privy. "Oh, Bob," he called.

"What?"

"Come in here." He came through the house.

"I don't want you going out to the privy again at night, you hear?"

"Yes."

Bob followed the old man back to the kitchen. "Here's a pan," the old man said. "You use that, you see?"

Bob was silent.

"You pee in this. Then in the morning I'll throw it out. Don't you go outside, you hear? At night them wolves might come around," and as the old man said it, he was pleased by the sound of it—"*might* come around"—and he knew they wouldn't come back. They had been here once, and that was that. It was one of them one-time things that you can later look back at and shake your head because it was a pretty rough time, but now it's over.

Bob went back to bed and was snoring in a minute, and the old man went up to his room and went to bed.

After a while, though, he got up and put on his overalls and shoes, just in case. Tonight he would sleep with one eye open, just in case. But he was confident the wolves were by now twenty, thirty miles away, and as he walked away into sleep he could nearly see the wolves going over a hill, far down the road, not one of them looking back over its shoulder at him.

"Oh God, no. Please, no," he whispered and opened his eyes as wide as he could.

They were running around the house.

He heard them running along the side of the house, then their claws clattered as they loped across the front porch, then he heard them cross the back porch.

Slowly he sat on the side of the bed, remembering he had left on his overalls and shoes but now angry with his carefulness, as if his leaving them on had somehow brought them back, and wearily he reached down to the floor, found the gun, and he stood up. The thudding of their feet and the clatter of their claws were now making a din that shook the house, and he walked without aiming himself, though habit led him from the bedroom into the front room, to the closed door. He stood there, a few feet from them, separated by the door, and he pictured their long gray bodies stretching as they raced across the porch, their long red tongues hanging out the sides of their mouths, and he leaned his forehead against the door, as if he would hold it closed that way, and the shotgun was tremendously heavy, and the darkness shifted as if the little house and the flat fields were slowly tilting—everything would soon start slowly sliding—and he tried to lick his lips but his mouth and tongue were dry, and his mouth hung open. He tried to call Bob, but he had no voice, it was buried under the thudding of their feet, the prancing of their claws on the porch . . .

Then silence.

He waited, thinking perhaps he was asleep, that he had dreamed and was now free from the dream and in the cool lake of sleep.

But he was still standing, his forehead numb against the door, the shotgun slipping from his cold hands.

He straightened up, got a grip on the gun and lifted it, and he turned.

At the rear of the house the back door and the screen door were wide open. Bob had gone out to the privy and he had left both doors open and as the old man stood looking through the house it was a great distance, an endless corridor, and beyond the door, outside the house, he saw a wolf coming toward him, running across the yard toward the back door, its head slowly, steadily bobbing up and down as it ran, though its eyes didn't lose his, as if their eyes were at the ends of a golden wire that was reeling up faster and faster, and then the wolf was on the back porch and across it and through the door, and the wolf was suddenly much larger, enormous, its shoulders brushing both sides of the door, and it was now in the kitchen, its footsteps heavy, and with each long stride the wolf was larger and larger until it was the biggest thing the old man had ever seen, and the old man lifted the gun to his shoulder and pulled both triggers and the shotgun knocked him back as the blast blew out the roof and walls and a bright red mouth of fire gaped through the darkness and the old man floated away into a low moan soft as a howl coming from a mile away and the old man listened to the moaning as he slowly spun away and he vaguely recognized words forming in the moan, words no wolf could ever utter unless perhaps it was a wolf that had shared the darkness of a blind man's life.

With the first warm breeze of morning he left him and went out the front door, not shutting it behind him, and walked down to the road, and out of habit he held his hand out as he always did when Bob led him. Finding the road, he turned to the right and, head lifted, his eyes open, he walked slowly at first, then faster, following the wide smooth rut, and at the bend he followed the turn without once losing the rut. Then further on he was in the coolness where the road passed the woods, and he heard its heavy silence cut by the clear song of a bird, and he stopped. He felt the wood's cool breath on his face, and he stood there so long he felt time passing, felt it by the increasing warmth of the sun.

He turned from the woods and walked on, following the rut, and he heard them trotting along behind him.

When he stopped, they stopped. He knew they would follow him all the way to Avery's, and they did.

SATISFACTION

A plastic *Vikki* is pinned above her left breast, her uniform is tight, shiny black, the cafe is yellow, everything—countertop, stools, walls, floor. Vikki leans against the pie case, her arms folded, round-shouldered. She is thinking, staring out the window at the empty street, her water-gray face pinching her eyes nearly closed, her lips pouting, curling down at the corners with exaggerated, childish repugnance. She is convinced that she is not in good health, lately she thinks about death but it is difficult, vague, and vast, for she is young and has not known anyone who died. But lately she has taken to thinking she is maybe dying. She knows for certain she is losing herself, maybe it is from working the graveyard shift, the longer she works it the more she'll lose.

The cook looks out the slot from the kitchen, his head moving from left to right, then disappearing. From what can be seen of him, he resembles Jimmy Durante—tightly wrinkled forehead, button eyes, huge veiny nose.

A tall man enters—swift, gliding—and sits at the counter before the door shuts behind him. He wears an orange nylon windbreaker and a red shirt, open at the throat. His lean, canine face has the strained but satisfied look of a young man who has laughed too much and now, to relax his aching face, has come off to look at nothing. "Hello," he says, his voice becoming yellow.

The waitress moves from the pie case and comes down the counter. She doesn't look at him but to his left, as if at someone beside him.

"Coffee," he says and smiles. His mouth is big, his teeth large and square. His nostrils flare when he smiles.

She brings the coffee and says, looking toward the door, "Twenty-one cents," and holds out her hand, a small white hand, a nice little hand, the fingers carefully, precisely shaped.

After she puts the money in the cash register, she leans against the pie case and stares straight ahead, not at him, not out the window, not at the clock which seems stopped at 3:22, the second hand fixed like the finger of an old man who, now that he has everyone's attention, has forgotten what he was going to say. The cook looks out, the large nose sliding from left to right down the slot. The young man sips his coffee and his eyes slowly move from the sneakers Vikki wears, up her legs, thighs, across her belly and breasts, to her petulant, preoccupied lips. Then slowly down again.

He finishes his coffee, remains sitting there, motionless, staring at her. Then he moves off the stool without making a sound and, pausing at the door to look back (she is staring at the floor), he goes out.

The street is empty, the air warm. The young man crosses the street and sits on the fender of a car, smoking. The building tops gradually become distinct against the gray morning sky. Black quick birds slice the air, they dip, strike straight up into the sky.

When her replacement arrives, Vikki leaves and walks up the sidewalk, not swinging her arms, her back bent. She doesn't carry a purse, her carefully made fingers curl like soft claws.

She turns up a narrow street with cars parked on both sides, and it so happens that as she does, the first sounds of the city move across the sky, a rumbling larger and steadier than thunder. She appears not to notice the sound or feel the subtle quaking under her feet as the city becomes itself, as if at that precise moment all the machines were switched into motion, all the trucks hit the street, all people leaned up and, with their eyes and mouths open wide, for the first time that day emitted themselves against the sky.

But no other people stir on this narrow street. The dense, dark apartment houses wait within windows recessed with grand formality in niches encrusted with scrolls and concrete foliage, the windowpanes themselves black and narrow like old men falling backward.

Vikki goes down the sidewalk, silent in her sneakers. Climbs the steps of a building, slips into the dark foyer.

The young man stops inside the doorway, listens. He hears the soft scuff of her shoes on the stairs and, looking up the stairwell, he sees a small white thing, her hand, sliding along the rail.

On the top floor there are three doors. On one an engraved card says "Rulla." On the next a triangular scrap of paper, the corner of a newspaper, glued to the center of the door, says, printed in pencil, "Mr. and Mrs. Stums." "Nadine Grune" is written in red crayon on the third door.

He opens that door and goes into the kitchen, dark, cluttered, the top of the stove piled with dishes and pots, food darkening in them. A path passes through sacks of garbage, empty cans staring at the wall where a calendar hangs beside a chalk plaque three feet long showing The Last Supper in brightly colored bas-relief, the faces of the diners jocundly pink above their tidy russet breards.

The path leads to a small room full of cardboard boxes, gaping suitcases seeming frozen in attempts to retch forth the clothes in them. A woman appears in the doorway to the next room.

She wears a brown robe and a halo of stiff gray hair. Thin, angular, above her square wide shoulders her long neck stretches to a face small as the waitress's, though there is no pout on her lips. "What do you want?"

"I know your daughter," he says. "I've come to see her."

She looks over her shoulder into the room. "Who is this?"

The young man moves quickly forward and sticks his head into the room, touching the woman's shoulder. "Hi," he says to the waitress sprawling, still in her uniform, on a purple easy chair before a t.v. set that isn't turned on. A large bed, unmade, tilts toward the center of the room. A narrow high window, uncurtained and unshaded, hides in a corner. The floor is covered with sweaters, skirts, underwear.

The waitress looks up, her face dark gray, lips protruding, her eyes half-closed.

"I'm Larry Sloper," he says, turning to the mother. He isn't smiling, though his face is intense, excessive. He nods toward the waitress: "We met last night at the cafe."

The mother's eyes move quickly, wary and indecisive. She then looks off. "Well," she says. She turns to Larry, her eyes now sharp, aggressive. "But what do you want?"

"Oh." He laughs. "Maybe we could talk."

Her eyes crinkle, then her face attempts an expression of openness, generosity, as if she has decided his words are exactly what she was hoping for. She smiles, demonstrating how wide her mouth can stretch, and showing that her teeth are good and that her tongue, though very wide and actually too long for her mouth, is a bright pink, healthy tongue. Clearly, she is a woman who likes to open her mouth and does it often, and clearly she likes showing men her mouth.

She turns, touches her hand to her hair as if one pat could put it in order. "Vikki has lots of friends," she says.

"Yes," Larry says, glancing at the waitress. She sits with her legs out straight on her heels, her skirt half up her thighs. She stares at the t.v. Larry nods. "I know she has lots of friends. And maybe," he turns slowly to her mother, "she has lovers as well."

The mother closes her mouth, the lips tighten, her eyes narrow. "I don't know what you mean." She shakes her head. "I don't know what you say that for. I don't . . ."

"Some coffee maybe," Larry says brightly.

She frowns, then says low, absently, "All right," and goes to the kitchen.

Larry stands with his hands on his hips, looking down at Vikki. "Well," he says.

He goes over to the bed and lies down, crossing his legs at the ankles. Above, he sees the thin landscape of cracks and stains which Vikki and her mother start off each day seeing.

"Go away," Vikki says. "I'm tired. I'm sick. I want to go to bed."

Larry sits up slowly. "Let me do something and then I'll leave. One thing." They look at each other in the reflection of the t.v. screen.

She shakes her head. "I don't let people do things."

"Let me kiss you one time and I'll leave."

"I don't let people kiss me."

"One time only. Just"–he snaps his fingers.

"No."

"All right. I'll kiss your mother."

She is silent, her eyes nearly closed. She shakes her head in the t.v. screen.

"Your mother likes me," Larry whispers, "I can tell. She likes me a lot. When she comes back I'll let you see what I can do. I'll let you see my stuff."

"No." Vikki leans forward and turns to face him around the back of the chair. "I'll let you kiss me if you'll go away."

"Ah ha! You know I'm right about that, don't you? You know your mother will let me kiss her. And everything else, too. Don't you?"

"No. I don't know that at all. I just want you to go away."

Larry goes to Vikki and takes her hand. It is warm, small. "All right," he says and leans down. She doesn't close her eyes but watches as he puts his mouth to hers. Her pouting lips are soft. He smells her lips, mouth, face, hair. Still holding his mouth to hers, he slowly kneels. He puts his hands on her knees and pressing slightly opens her legs as far as the tight skirt allows.

They hear her mother coming from the kitchen. Larry gets to his feet and turns to the window.

"It's difficult to live these days," he says, looking at the street below. "It's difficult to get satisfaction." He looks at the mother. She has combed her hair and put on dark red lipstick, making her lips heart-shaped. She hands Larry a cup of coffee. "A person needs the right people," Larry says, "and the right place. This is a good place." He extends his hand and with a slow gesture covers the room from the window, along the wall and the t.v. set and Vikki, and along the inside wall. "I like it here." He sips his coffee and sets it down. "I could get satisfaction. Have you ever thought of taking in roomers?"

"Hear that, Vikki?" the mother says.

Vikki doesn't answer.

"My," the mother says. "Roomers. My."

Larry stares at her and leans forward, not moving his feet, and because he is tall he can lean three, four feet without losing his balance: he leans toward the mother, his face hovering near her hair and face while she looks up at him, her eyes rather large. "Do you want to?" Larry says.

"Uh," the mother says.

Larry's mouth is open, almost smiling. "I told Vikki you would let me."

"Oh," the mother says. "You did." She nods slowly. "My, imagine that."

Larry puts his hands on her hips. He can feel the muscle and bone in them, through the thin bathrobe. She is wearing nothing under the robe. Larry smiles, pulls her closer, she moves against him, they stand pelvis to pelvis. "Do you know what satisfaction is?" Larry says low.

"No."

"Satisfaction is your mouth full and both hands full and you look out the window and see it coming down the street." He waits. "Now. Satisfaction, dear lady, is your anal asshole."

The mother's eyes drift, they almost close as if she is gone. Then slowly she shakes her head no. Her eyes open, blink, she wrinkles her nose, twitching her nostrils, and a smug expression comes to her face. "I don't like dirty talk." Her expression is one of great contentment. "Dirty talk gets my goat and I don't like it. Dirty talk and dirty people who talk dirty, they get my goat."

Slowly, with some effort, Larry blushes. The mother nods, she likes that. Vikki turns on the t.v.

The mother pushes Larry, he releases her hips. She is smiling vengefully, her eyes keen. "I think this Larry fellow has bitten off more than he can chew," the mother says, going to the chair where Vikki is slumped down, her head propped on one hand. The t.v. screen is red and blue. The people's hands and faces are blue, everything else is sizzling red.

"I. . ." Larry says, still blushing. "I get carried away. I apologize for that."

"Well, now," the mother says, one hand on her hip. "That's more like it." She shakes her head, standing across the room from him. "We don't allow just anything around here. Let's hear it again. I don't think Vikki heard it. You kind of mumbled on it."

"Okay." He looks down at the floor, at wool skirts, panties, brassieres. "I apologize," he says louder than before.

Then he looks up at her from under his brows. The mother is smiling, her lips, cheeks, her eyes up-lifted in accomplishment.

With a hand still on her hip, she lifts the other and touches her hair. As she does, she slightly rolls her hips, twists her shoulders. She licks her lips. "Do you per chance have a cigarette?"

"Sure." He takes out his pack and she comes across the room, a hand still on her hip, putting one foot directly ahead of the other, swaying her hips, her eyes half-closed, dreamy. She takes a cigarette and he strikes a match. His hand is shaking. She puts her hand on his, looking him in the eye. "Now," she whispers. "What was that you said?" He smells her breath, a brown wet meaty smell with tobacco on top.

"I apologize," he says.

"No," she whispers. "That other. You know."

"Oh." He nods. He whispers, "Your anal asshole."

The words go into her through her eyes, opening the pupils, her expression widening somberly, even mournfully, her lips under the expression of wide, flaccid expansion becoming full and soft. "Do you know any others?" she whispers. "Just like that? Do you know any for the. . ." She rolls her glance down, then up to his eyes. "The. . ." She looks down again, then up, and soundlessly lips what looks like *boots.*

He shakes his head.

A single frown line creases the great plane of her forehead. She lifts a hand and with a fingernail taps one of her breasts.

"Oh," Larry says.

She smiles weakly, crookedly, as if things are sinking deep into her and taking her down with them. "Well?"

He nods, his eyes closing, his nostrils large. She is looking up his nostrils while waiting. He leans forward and whispers in her face: "Bitten tits."

At first, nothing. But she soundlessly repeats it and he sees her eyes deepening. Her eyes lose focus as if she is not being taken in the direction she expected to go but is reminded of some matter, old and unresolved, which only infrequently comes back, surprising her each time with the force and amazing power it still has.

"How do you like it?" Larry says.

"Oh." She is vague. "Yes. I just. . ."

"There's one close to it," he says. "Bleeding bitch tits."

She waits, licks her lips. Shakes her head. "Not . . . not as good as the other one."

He turns and goes to the window, stands with his hands in his pockets. She follows him and stands to the side and slightly behind him. "What's wrong?" she whispers. Then louder, urgent, "Aren't there any more? I mean . . . come on."

He glances over his shoulder, then back out the window. "There's plenty of time. Remember, satisfaction is you see it coming down the street."

She nods impatiently. "But we don't *need* to wait. You can tell me some more."

"I just told you one and you didn't even hear it."

"What?"

"The street."

She looks out the window. Below, a man and a woman walk toward the corner.

The mother frowns, trying to see in them.

"What is satisfaction?" Larry says.

"It's. . ."

"You don't listen." He shakes his head. "I shouldn't even be up here."

Then she says in a rush, "You see it coming on the street. But that's not as good."

"That's because you haven't tried."

"Haven't *tried*?" She laughs. "I'm fifty-four years old and that's haven't tried."

"You haven't tried." He turns again and says low but sharply as if hitting her with sharp little hammers, "It's satisfaction, right? Big *S*, big twisty *S*. You want, right? And you've had it twice now. Right?"

"Twice?"

"With me. Don't tell me you've forgot already."

She shakes her head. "No." She swallows. "I won't ever forget. You're right. I'm sorry. Don't. . ." She can't say it. He stares at her. "Don't go away," she whispers. "Say you won't."

"For now."

She leans against him, puts her face against his shoulder, cries.

He watches t.v. with Vikki and doesn't like the show. "There's too much face," he says.

Vikki looks at him, then back to the set.

"Close-ups are good only once, twice a day," he says. "More than that and it's all face, sloppy."

"If you don't like it don't. . ." Her voice sinks.

"What?"

"Don't watch," she says, raising her voice with effort.

"Which do you like? The blue men, the mustaches?" She doesn't answer. "The young woman with three blue diseases?"

"I can't hear what they say if you. . ." sinking.

"What?"

"If you don't shut up."

"You want them to get married and have babies?"

She doesn't answer. But there rises from her body an emanation, a smell. Not the same smell she brings home from work in her hair, on her skin—a yellow smell of fried meat grease and cigarette smoke.

The emanation that rises from her body is partly electrical. The cells of her body speak out, their little voices tight and gritty, certain.

"Babies!" Larry says.

She is sweating, all over at once. She kicks off her sneakers and wiggles her toes.

"How many babies do you want?" Larry asks.

"I want to watch. . ."

"Ah. You want to watch it on t.v. Women having babies all day."

"Oh," Vikki says and bends to the side, drawing her legs under her.

Larry stands before the t.v. set. Like blue and red X-ray the set shines through his trousers, showing he wears no undershorts and also showing his personal member in distinct profile. "Let's talk," he says, putting his hands in his pockets. Watching what his hands are doing, she doesn't hear a word he says.

"She has lovers," her mother says, leaning over and resting her arms on the back of Vikki's chair. "You were right, Larry."

"Shh," he says. "Don't distract."

Vikki hears some of what Larry is telling: "Thus prepared for the nuptial doings, the maiden is led, well-dazed and oiled, shining in the torchlight. . ."

"Is this it?" Vikki says loudly and clearly. "Just this?" It is her message. Uttered into the squibble-squabble of the t.v. and Larry's scenario, it is heard by no one, Vikki herself hardly hears.

It is a big moment that doesn't get off the ground. Except in the moments that follow, Vikki is full of herself, new and brilliant, ready for something really important.

But it passes, she sinks, is gone again, is just there inside 103 pounds of Nadine Grune's daughter, in a shiny black uniform, being ineluctably drawn to Larry—for by now she is wholly in love, taken with his personal member which she believes is extra-big, a whopper in fact, though every one she sees seems extra-big.

"Golly!" Vikki says and jumps from her chair, dizzy as a witch, and reaches in as Larry unzips his fly.

***

By two p.m. the movement and noise of the city reach a level that keeps the building in constant vibration. In the apartment the three people lie motionless in bed, Larry Sloper in the middle, the sheet pulled up to their chins. They wait, as if consciously studying the traffic, the sounds of voices, the sky's flaring blue and quick white. It would appear the three intently listening people are waiting for a signal. Their faces are expressionless ovals. Their breathing is much slower than most people's, and as the afternoon wears on, their noses become sharp, as do the noses of people who must attend too closely to everything around them. Now and then as if playing a droll game they blink in unison.

At about six p.m. the city's noise ebbs and the sky chameleonlike within itself transpires from flat and aimless blue to pensive gray. Then night is everywhere at once. A horn blares on the street below, and the three people hidden in the bed are startled by the sound.

Vikki gets up and puts on her sneakers and her uniform. She turns on a small yellow-shaded floor lamp, its dim bulb makes the room cavernous with shadows. She switches on the t.v. and stands before it, combing her hair. When she is done, she turns off the t.v. but leaves the lamp burning. She goes to the bed, her mother and Larry lie looking up at her. Vikki leans over and kisses Larry, then her mother. "Good-night," Vikki whispers.

She leaves the room, then far off the hall door shuts.

PATSY O'DAY IN THE WORLD

The windows floated in the water of dawn and like a murky tide gray crossed the ceiling. Soft arms of gray slowly reached down into the room, gray bellies bulged from the ceiling until the room, a dark pool in which Patsy floated on her back, was filled with the same cold gray as the ceiling, the windows, the sky.

She got up and went to the window. Far below, the street was a black and gray canal. As always, there were people on the wide sidewalks. She opened a window and leaned out, as though she would call down and tell them it was all right for them to start now, she was awake, she was ready. But she didn't call down to them–it was cold and she closed the window and watched them, four men. Two stood in a dark doorway, another with folded arms leaned on a parking meter, the fourth sat on the curb. She leaned her forehead against the cold glass trying to see if perhaps one of them was Peter Gone. Yesterday he told her he would come back last night, but he hadn't. When they left she always wondered if she would see them again. But Peter Gone would come back. She was sure he would. She knew him–*knew* him. And she knew other people in the same deep way, a mysterious certainty that she never tried to explain to herself or anyone else. But she *knew,* and with this special knowledge she could love Peter Gone, with his soft and lonely eyes, and she would help him.

She went back to the mattress and lay down, her hands folded under her head, and she felt herself slipping out of the gray when she heard footsteps in the hall. Then the door opened. Mr. Moluska stuck his head in, looked around the big empty room, then stepped quickly in and shut and locked the door behind him. He was wearing the same old suit he always wore, gray and slick, and his wide-brimmed black felt hat which made his pale, long face even more weird. Coming toward the mattress, not looking at her yet but around the room at the posters and pictures covering the walls, he took off his coat, shirt, trousers. tisking as he frowned at the blue and orange dayglo "Up Nixon With The ABM." The last thing he took off was his big black hat, and as he did he looked at Patsy and smiled, his old blue lips drawing back from his shiny teeth. Then he took out his teeth, put them in his hat, and set it beside the mattress. His old gray body jiggled rubbery as he knelt down on the mattress beside her.

He put his teeth back in his mouth and put on his hat. He sat crossed-legged, reached out and patted her. "I'm still like a young man, eh?"

"You sure are, Mr. Moluska."

"You know how I do it?"

"How?"

"I'm sixty years old and I never done nothing I didn't really want to do. You know what I'm saying?"

She nodded.

"That's the answer, chickie. You see this?" He held himself up for her to see, as if she hadn't already seen quite enough for one morning. "My friend is sixty years old like me. But it don't act it, right? It thinks it's thirty, forty years old. Maybe younger even." He nodded, looking down at himself fondly.

He glanced around the room at the posters and loudly glaring faces—saintly Chés, awed Vietnamese children naked amid smoking rubble, Malcom X staring rigidly at Mr. Moluska and Patsy. "Now this kind of thing . . ." Mr. Moluska shook his head. "This makes my friend sad. You know? You've been here what is it two weeks? and already look at you." He shook his head. "And the one before you the same way. It's no good. Marry and be a wife. Stop all the groping. And that on your stomach. Cute. But it's stupid. Believe me you'll regret it," and he leaned forward to take another look at the dime-sized yellow butterfly tattooed near her navel.

"But after you there'll be another one and I'll see it all over again. What's your name I forgot."

"Patsy O'Day."

He nodded. "I'll forget again. About the time I learn your name they send another one." He turned to the posters again. "I told the last one not to put up these things." He looked at Patsy. "But she done it anyway. Why? So I tell her all right put them up but put them up with little pins, you know, those little pins that have the plastic ends on them, make little tiny holes. But no. She puts them up with the Scotch tape and she nails them up with nails this long. You know what it does to the walls?"

"When are you going to do something about the window panes, Mr. Moluska?" Patsy said softly.

"The window panes look at them you break them out for me to put more in, is that it?" He got up and strode across the room. Some of the small panes were broken out completely and repalced by squares of cardboard. Others were patched with black tape. "Two or three girls back I put in all new panes and the next day I come up to see how they are and there's three, four panes broke out already and the girl says they had a big rally and the futz broke out the windows with their billy clubs."

"Fuzz."

"Eh?"

"Fuzz, Mr. Moluska."

"Fuzz to you too, chickie. You got a sweet box and a big heart too, you share, but no complaints about the window panes or I tell Mr. Russell it's quits and I'll move out your headquarters to the sidewalk. And your fuzz'll help me too, believe me."

Patsy sat in the middle of the mattress and watched as Mr. Moluska put on his clothes.

"What you say to that?" he said.

She smiled. "All right, Mr. Moluska."

He looked away, then quickly back at her as if he thought she would laugh at him when he turned away.

"Well I'll go now," he said.

"All right."

"You're a good chickie."

"Yes. You said."

He nodded. "Yes. Well, bye-bye."

"Bye-bye."

He unlocked the door, stuck his head out and looked up and down, then stepped out into the hall. His head popped back in. "Aren't you going to lock this door?"

She shook her head.

"You should lock your door. It's a city law. It fights crime. So lock it."

"I'm expecting friends. If I lock it I'll just have to unlock it again."

"'Expecting friends.' Believe me, chickie, you'll not see sixty. Not you." He waited for her to speak. She didn't. So he shrugged and shut the door.

The three young men had just sneaked back in from Canada and they told Patsy they were bounders—they demonstrated by locking arms and bounding across the floor with giant lunging hops, all six feet landing at the same time, shaking the room, the floor cracking and making splitting sounds. Patsy laughed and expected the floor to fall through. When they fell and rolled laughing on the floor, they heard the Cubans yelling in the apartment below. Patsy was pouring cups of broth for them as they sat on pillows on the floor telling her about the headquarters in Canada, and Senor Yero burst in shouting Spanish and shaking two big hunks of plaster in Patsy's face. He was a bony little man and his rage was pitiful—Patsy wanted to cry and put her arms around him. His whole body trembled as he shouted at her and shook the crumbling plaster at her and then at the three boys sitting on the floor, and he spluttered out a word or two of English. Tears ran down his cheeks and Patsy put her arms around him. He pushed her away, but he had calmed somewhat and Patsy apologized and made promises. "No hable Espanol," one of the fellows said and waved good-bye to him.

Then people started calling and Patsy was on the phone for a solid hour while the three bounders slept on the floor. Megan came around to leave a note for Bill if he showed up on his way to the new resistance office. The man upstairs started up his big electric sewing machine and a snow of fine powder started falling from the ceiling. The sewing machine woke the three bounders—they thought it was an airplane. Patsy phoned out some telegrams, charging them to one of the numbers Russell had listed in the big book Patsy used.

Tracy, Ralph, Max, and Louis came for a meeting, but the rest of their committee didn't come. Thanking Patsy for messing things up again—for she had set up the meeting—they left. They hadn't been gone ten minutes before George, Bob, and Woody, the rest of the committee, came in and they got mad at Patsy too. They were yelling at her, they were going to tear up the place, and the three boys who were back from Canada woke, thought there was going to be a fight, and started slipping for the door, the last of them apologizing to Patsy for not staying around, explaining hastily that right now they couldn't afford a confrontation that might involve the fuzz because they had word the FBI was just two hops behind them. When George, Bob, and Woody heard that, they stopped yelling at Patsy and started talking to the three bounders, found they had mutual friends, and George, Bob, and Woody knew how they could help the three fellows make it to San Francisco, if they wanted to go to San Francisco—and sure enough they *did* want to go to San Francisco. Patsy made more broth and they all sat down. Woody said he had some things to do out in San Francisco and maybe he should go with them. He knew a ride they could get out of Philly with a friend of his who was, he said, a groovy spade, but they would have to let him know fast. Patsy phoned down to Philly, and while Woody was talking to his groovy spade friend, more people came in, many meetings were taking place, and Patsy was cooking broth for everyone. Some people who had been evicted brought their things in and rigged up their stereo tape set and started playing Chinese music. They had a tv set and they turned on a soap opera with the sound off. The sewing machine upstairs jangled the picture, zagging the people in half. A girl with freckles passed Patsy a joint. Everyone was full of peace, and Patsy was happy because they were. Then Peter Gone walked in.

Peter had been on speed for two weeks and for the last two days Patsy was the only person he could talk to and the only person he could bear to even *look* at. He cried, head down, his narrow bird shoulders slumped, his arms tight at his sides as he stood against her. They went into the bathroom to talk.

"Who are all those people?" he said. His eyes were gray. She had noticed they were getting grayer every day.

"They're good people, Peter. They're like you and me."

"Who was that big guy?"

"I don't know who you mean."

"The one . . . " He shook his head. He couldn't go on.

"Peter, Peter, Peter," she said softly and put her arms around him. He put his face against her neck. Soon her neck was wet. She lifted his face, it was wet with tears, and she kissed him. She held him and kissed him a long time, not moving her face but gently kissing him again and again, and she felt him relaxing.

"Do you feel better?"

"A little."

"Do you want to lie down?"

"There's too many people."

"There's a place upstairs."

Patsy led Peter through the room, which was now much quieter than before, everyone was smoking and some were watching the people getting cut up on tv, and the stereo was playing sitar music. Woody was still on the phone to his friend in Philly.

The room where Patsy took Peter was two floors up, and two floors up it was another world. The long, brown and gray corridor was narrower than the other halls. The doors looked as if they hadn't been opened in years. Patsy wondered if the people who lived up here ever came out.

They went down the hall and Patsy glanced at Peter. His face was out of shape with an awful frown. It was dead white and crumpled into mean little lines. Suddenly he was a pitiful little old man years and years older than Mr. Moluska.

The room wasn't locked—there was no reason to lock it. It was small and bare—no bathroom, no closet, no sink. The only thing in the room was a small window in the outside wall. Patsy slowly shut the door behind them. She had brought a blanket, and she spread it on the floor. She sat down and held up her hand to Peter Gone. He looked down at her, his eyes gray and vacant. He stared at her as if he had just seen her, as if she had appeared out of nowhere and he was wondering where she came from, who she was. He slowly sat down beside her.

"I saw . . . " he started, stopped, shook his head, his eyes clenched, his head hanging. Then he opened his eyes and quickly looked around, looked right at Patsy. "Do you know what I saw?"

"What did you see?"

"I was just going down the street and . . . I saw . . . " Again he stopped.

"You saw many things, didn't you, Peter?"

He stared at her a long time. "Eating," he whispered. "They were eating. Everyone was eating and I stood and looked at them. They just kept on eating and I stood on the sidewalk and watched them doing it."

"It's all right, Peter."

He was still staring at her, his eyes while she lookied into them, seeming to become even grayer, as if deep within them a vortex was swirling, slowly and steadily emptying all the color out of him. "Poor baby," Patsy said, and kissed him.

She unbuttoned his jacket and started taking it off. He moved his arms, assisting her. She unbuttoned his shirt and took it off. His body was soft, small, and again Patsy thought of Mr. Moluska and his soft fat body: it occurred to her that Mr. Moluska carried another person around under his skin, a person like Peter. Maybe Mr. Moluska had absorbed a young man into himself, absorbed all but for one vital part of the young man which Mr. Moluska allowed to remain on the outside so he could use it on the chickies.

Patsy pushed gently on Peter Gone and he lay back on the blanket. She took off her sweater and jeans while he stared up at her, his gray eyes large. She leaned over him, put the nipple of her left breast into his mouth, and he closed his eyes.

She left Peter in the room, asleep at last, and she went back downstairs. When he woke in the tiny gray room he would wonder where he was, he might even be scared—it might be . . . bad. But Patsy couldn't stay with him until he woke. He might sleep for two days.

Back in the apartment some people had left, some new ones had come, and in the middle of the room stood two big Negroes very elegant in black leather, posing with their hands on the hips of their skin-tight slacks. One of them looked coldly at Patsy as she came in. The look was imperious, murderous. She shivered and went straight to him. "Hi," she said.

He stared at her and his frown intensified by the tightening of his eyes.

"Hey, Patsy," it was Woody. "I was talking to my buddy in Philly and this chick and a guy started hassling me about who I am and where I'm calling from and what the number is and what the address is and who has the phone, who pays for it, so I told them I was at a pay phone and then it just cuts like dead, man, and I can't even get a dial tone, you know?" As he ended he was speaking up to the queen, who was a foot taller than he. The queen stared back at him without blinking.

"Well," Patsy said, "I'll have to let Russell know so he can get in a new line."

The people who had been evicted started moving their stuff out—one of them, a fat fellow in black pajamas and a Panama hat, had found a new place. That was good, because Patsy was running out of the little packages for making broth—and then she discovered she was now in fact all out because while she was upstairs with Peter someone had walked out with the last of the little packages.

It was raining now and everyone except the two black queens lay looking out the windows. It was just a shower and then the sun came out and, now in the west, shone through the windows and people stripped down and went to sleep in the sun.

"What's your name?" One of the black queens stood looking down at Patsy. Maybe he was thinking of stepping on her.

"Patsy. What's your name?"

"Your hands are bleeding."

She smiled, held up her hand, and looked at her fingernails. She nodded. "I chew my fingernails. When I was a kid I guess I never got enough of it and . . . "

"Russell say the headquarters gotta move outa here." He slowly lifted a hand and pointed a huge finger at her face. "He say you *done*."

The others had turned and were watching. "The headquarters are moving, Patsy?" someone asked.

"Russell always tells Bird McWilliams and Bird McWilliams tells me about any messages he has," Patsy answered, looking to the side, then up at the queen.

He stared down at her. "He say you *done*."

Patsy smiled. "Groovy. I'm done." She nodded her head brightly. "So Bird McWilliams will come and tell me. Okay?"

"No bird about it. You just get your ass out." He looked around at them. "All of you. Out."

"No," Patsy said, still smiling, though the smile was numb on her face and she calmly wondered if he would hit her or kick her, and she decided she would rather he hit her for if he did he would hit her face, but if he kicked her she knew he would kick her in a breast. But she knew she had no choice—he would kick her, and while she waited, telling herself she wouldn't close her eyes until she actually saw him starting to move, someone across the room spoke.

"Friend." That was all he said. They all turned and looked at him. He was a little guy with long red hair. In his Jockey shorts he sat cross-legged in the sun and he held a big black revolver. And he didn't say anything else, he just looked at the queen.

The queen squinted, his black face ascending in folds and lines, as if to shield him from the little black eye at the end of the gun barrel.

There was a long silence. They listened to the sewing machine upstairs.

The queen curled his lips back in a strange smile, looked down at Patsy—she smiled back at him—and a thin jet squirted from between his teeth and hit her face.

Not wiping her face, she nodded and said softly, "All right," and the queen turned slowly. He and the other one walked out the door and didn't shut it behind them.

"Paulie," the red-headed guy with the gun said. One of the others who still had his clothes on jumped up and crossed the room, paused at the door, and went out.

Several of them started talking all at once, but the guy with the gun said sharply, "Cool it," and they were silent again.

Paulie came back smiling broadly. "They're gone." The young man with the gun touched the barrel to his forehead in a salute and stuck it under a pile of clothes beside him.

Patsy got up and went over and kissed the red-headed guy. He told her his name was Phillip.

Then some girls came in with two big brown sacks of doughnuts. They were hard but good, and then it was raining again and everyone lay back and watched the gray rain streak the windows and soak the squares of cardboard that replaced the broken panes.

People were coming and going. The rain stopped, the sun was out again, and after the darkness of the shower it was as if this were the beginning of a new day. The sun shone against the windows and Patsy turned and while Phillip talked to her, his voice seeming to come from far away, she looked toward the windows and at the sky, and as she was facing the sun on the glistening panes something flashed by the window—white, quick, a large pale pillow with arms and legs stuck out at the corners—and Phillip was saying ". . . the other chicks . . . " and she saw the flash just as he said *other,* the streak snipping between the syllables, and by the time he said *chicks*, Patsy heard the first surprised gasps and the first scream of a girl standing with her hand on the window sill, and then people were talking all at once—"Did you *see* that." "I saw it but what was it?"—and Patsy knew what it was, and the girl still standing there with her hand on the window sill also knew what it was before someone said that it was Peter Gone, and someone said low, "Groovy. Peter's gone," and they were silent, as if what he said was profound, or as if it were a tricky punch line that they had to repeat several times to themselves before they could laugh. Then they were freed from the long silence when a girl said, "It's not funny, man," and the girl who screamed when she first saw him, screamed again and turned and looked at Patsy across the room and said, "I saw him *falling.* I saw his *face* as he was *falling.*" Some went to the window and tried to look down at the sidewalk, and as they did, Patsy stood up and in spite of herself she wondered if he would be on the sidewalk or if he had reached the street, and frowning she shook her head. But she couldn't leave it alone, and as she stood behind those who got to the window first she knew that he had hit the curb, and she closed her eyes and took a deep breath, for to have hit the curb was worse, much worse. Then they were all leaving the apartment, crowding at the door, Patsy with them, and she heard the girl talking in a shrill, disbelieving tone, "I saw his *face.* His eyes were open. He was falling with his *eyes* open," and a guy was holding her arm and talking back at her, into her face, trying to talk over her, to blur out her words with his, saying over and over to her in a voice trying for calmness but instead achieving an almost pedantic seesawing, the tone of a parent or a teacher being patient, "All right, so cool it. It's unimportant, dig? It's unimportant," and as Patsy was pushed along with them out the door and down the hall toward the stairs she wanted to tell the guy—who was a bore, she decided, a really big bore—that maybe it *was* important. How did *he* know what was important and what wasn't?

There was a hassle with the police and Mr. Moluska, and then that night the phone was working again and Patsy turned it over to a long-legged skinny blond named Gracie who had just arrived from Berkeley.

Patsy went for a walk and met a couple of fellows and went with them to a very crowded party in a basement apartment. After most of the people had left, she and one of the fellows, Roy, lay staring up at a slowly revolving amber glass ball hanging from the ceiling. She cried and told Roy about Peter Gone. "He was such a beautiful little guy, you know?" she said.

"With that name he like had a hex on him," Roy siad.

She talked about Peter for a long time and as she did she suddenly understood what she felt was a deep, sad mystery: Peter was beautiful—and because he was beautiful he had to do what he did. And the beauty justified what he did. Beauty justified everything. "Hold me," she whispered to Roy as the slow sweep of amber light moved over them, and he held her. "Mirrors watch people," she whispered. "One time that's what Peter told me," though he hadn't told her that at all. "Isn't that beautiful?"

"Heavy," Roy said.

They left the basement apartment and walked around for a while and went to an all-night place. They sat at the counter and watched the all-night freaks and weirdos, and Roy told Patsy about himself, talking about when he was a kid, and Patsy supposed he was trying to cheer her up but she couldn't get interested. She V-ed her fingers, smiled sadly at Roy, got off her stool at the counter, and left.

With her head down she walked, now and then looking up at the black windows of buildings. She wondered if anyone was sitting at one of those dark windows looking out, seeing her.

"I am becoming someone too," she said out loud. "The least a person can do is be someone." And she liked that. It gave her the warm glow of bravery.

She walked until the massive, solid hulks of night were etched into patterns and shapes by gray that slowly spilled into the city from the east. The silence was rumpled more and more frequently by the indistinct, submerged sounds of machinery like giants slowly coming to life.

She saw a man standing on a street corner. As she walked toward him he didn't turn or even lift his head. He was small and wore a shapeless coat. He stood with his head down so far Patsy thought he had gone to sleep staring at his feet. She stopped beside him. She looked down at his feet, then up at what she could see of his face, blotched by a gray and black stubble. At first she thought his eyes were closed. But then she saw his eyelids were cracked, though she couldn't see the eyes under them.

"You looking for a place to sleep, friend? I know a place just up the street about two . . ."

"Fuck off," he rasped.

"I just . . . "

"Fuck off."

She crossed the street and on the other side looked back at him. He still stood there with his head down.

She walked for a couple of hours and then went back to the apartment building. The building was awake, morning noises and voices rattling down the halls as she climbed the stairs. She walked down the hall, but the door to the apartment was locked.

She stared at the scars and gouges in the door. She knocked lightly.

"Go away." It was a man's voice, muffled though familiar.

"Come back later," a girl said.

She went back to the stairs and sat on the top step. She put her head on her knees and soon she was just short of sleep, in the gray whirl that could become either delirium or sleep, and she looked for Peter Gone and was sure he would come tumbling out of the gray billows and she was confident that now she would get the meaning—he would stand naked before her and with his unblinking gray eyes tell her all of the horror and beauty he had found, since now he knew everything. Smiling with his knowledge, he would turn her on . . .

But there was nothing. She slept perhaps, but fitfully, waking at the sound of her own voice though she hadn't heard what she said and couldn't remember to whom she thought she was speaking. She slept again, and woke when she heard the apartment door being unlocked. Mr. Moluska came out wearing his gray suit and his wide-brimmed black felt hat. He was nodding and saying goodbye to someone in the apartment. Then he shut the door, turned, and saw Patsy. He tipped his hat. "How's Gracie?" Patsy said flatly.

"Fine. A little skinny but she's a good girl." As he passed her he patted her shoulder. "Bye-bye," he said and started down the stairs.

"Bye-bye."

In the apartment Gracie, still naked, was talking on the phone. Patsy walked over to the windows and stood looking out.

"No . . . Listen . . . I didn't mean that. Just . . . Listen. Do this. Tell him you'll do it if he'll pay some of the gas, tell him five bucks, that's not too much . . . I know, so he's a prick, but you'd be a prick too if . . . So just a chance give him a chance, okay? Is that asking too much for Chrissake?"

Patsy went to the door. "Hey, kid," Gracie said and Patsy turned. "Wait a minute, okay?"

Patsy smiled and shook her head.

Gracie shrugged her bony shoulders and went back to talking on the phone.

On the street again Patsy stood on a corner watching the cars glide along with smooth, silent speed. A steady rumble throbbed in the streets, vibrating between the buildings. She walked down the street and around her pulsed the presence of people, and she stared at their faces, at their quick eyes, waiting for someone to look at her.

A LAMENT TO WOLVES

Again Ella's hands trembled. She looked away from Loren and the others, and put down her cup and saucer. She stood up, and they continued talking as she left the room.

In the kitchen she stood at the sink and looked out the window. Her hands were still. She saw his face, then, reflected gray in the window, and her hands trembled—the fingers tingling, cold, and a feeling like cold silk grazing the insides of her arms made her press them to her sides.

Her mother hobbled into the kitchen. "Well, Ella, I don't guess you and Edmond would consider staying over tonight."

"No," she said. "Edmond gets up even earlier on Mondays than on the rest of the week. He's got a truckload of lumber that's supposed to come up from Tennessee, and he's having some trouble with the hired hands. He just can't get them to work regular. And things pile up on weekends, so Mondays are bad."

Her mother went to the icebox as Ella spoke. Perhaps she listened to what Ella said. She got a big pitcher of buttermilk. "Mondays. Mondays always have been bad days for me. It was a Monday your daddy got killed, and it was a Monday I had my stroke, and. . ." She poured the buttermilk and held up the glass level with her old gray eyes. She stared at it as if she feared something was wrong with it.

She drank the whole glass of buttermilk without taking it from her thin-lipped, hard mouth. With the tip of her tongue she licked at the thick white moustache it left on her lip. Staring out the window, she said, "But it was Monday a week tomorrow that I got the telegram from Loren saying he was still alive and he was coming home at last."

For a moment Ella thought her mother was praying, for her breath wheezed and Ella could nearly hear the hissed whisper of the intense prayers her mother constantly uttered—though Ella had decided long ago, when she was a child, that they weren't truly prayers, that they weren't addressed to God but that they were just old-woman whispering. She wasn't talking to herself, she didn't even know herself what she was saying. She was just mumbling.

In the other room, Loren, his wife Ringo, and Edmond laughed loudly—Loren louder than the rest. They were laughing, Ella knew, at something Loren said. Ella's mother wiped off the buttermilk with the back of her hand and shook her head from side to side. "Thank God the boy's turned out good. He's a good man, like his daddy was." Ella stared out the window. "It's a miracle," her mother went on. "If you ask me, it's a miracle of God," and she was silent until the nervous movement of her lips resumed, the restless whispering.

"Well, let's go join the party," her mother said and she gave Ella a long look. And for a moment Ella was afraid of the knowing in her mother's look, afraid of what her mother knew. When her mother spoke again her tone was so low it was almost inaudible—as if it were coming from that remote level of the old woman's mumbling—so low Ella even thought it perhaps wasn't her mother's voice at all. "You're glad your brother has come home, aren't you, Ella?"

"Yes." She knew it was a terrible thing to admit.

"Yes. Good. We should be thankful."

He left the same day their father was killed in the orchard, and Ella had stood in the barnloft and looked out and she had seen her father running toward the farm and people were chasing him. No. No one had been chasing him. What she had seen and what she had dreamed were tangled like the dead limbs of the trees in the orchard, and when she thought of what happened her hands and arms ached, and Loren had hurt her, he had held her under water in the creek, straddled her, gripping her arms, and he held her under the water. He had kissed her and hurt her and held her under the water and then he went away and she was in the barn. . .

She followed her mother into the other room. Ella looked at Edmond. He sat listening to another of Loren's stories, and as Ella watched her husband, she saw his lips move slightly. Then his smile—the soft, boyish, gentle smile—as he laughed at Loren's story. She was afraid for Edmond, afraid for him to be here in the same room with Loren.

She sat down and tried not to listen.

"If you're a civilian employee you got it made. They can't get close to you because there ain't that many of you so you don't have to stay all in one place like the soldiers do, so we spread out, just wherever we want to be so it's good for us.

"And we can do all those other goodies that the military types can't, like Trick Three." His sharp eyes glistened. "We put up somethin and when we get done with it we wait around and if they're goona move in . . . we see if they're gonna move in or just squat out there and look, cause you can tell if they're out there, every time. I can smell em. I can smell them a thousand yards off.

"So we move off and wait and when they move in to take over the stuff we put in there, we zap it. Dynamite." He shook his huge, handsome head, his lips curled into a ferocious smile. "That's Trick Three. They set in the grass and let us build it and they go in and then we blow it up. We got lots of tricks like that. We call it tricks because they don't know what we're doin.

"Trick One is real nasty. We draw em in close when we're putting something up like pontoons and they're goin to jump us. See they think we don't know they're there, so they come in real close, right up to the water so we can't get away. They see we don't have no dogs, so they don't think we can know they're there, because the dogs can smell them, the Army has dogs with them, but we don't. Because I can smell them. I can smell them more good than the dogs can," he started chuckling, deep in his throat, and he looked at Ringo and the two of them laughed as if this part of the story had special meaning for them, and they laughed louder and louder, and Edmond (Like a boy, Ella thought, listening to a story about men and women and death, and laughing even though he doesn't understand) laughed and slapped his knee. "So they crowd up, see, and we're just standing around workin. They think. But in the shed we got a big auger and we drill in the bank down twenty feet and we got air tanks we dump in, and then we radio in air strikes and then we go in the shed and we go down in the hole with the air tanks." He swallowed. "Just about time they think they'll jump us, *splop*! they get the old napalm mufuck.

"That's Trick One. We done that a couple times."

Ringo—huge, hugely voluptuous, big-breasted, long-legged, blond, her face strangely large, bloated, as if it had never stopped growing—Ringo was nearly as large as Loren himself. Together in the room they seemed unnaturally immense, and if they wanted to, they could stand up and destroy everything—the furniture, the ceiling, the entire house—destroy it all by simply standing and lifting their arms.

Ringo told about the girl who did her hair at the beauty shop in Bon Dok. The girl sometimes came to work with bandages on her arms and feet. Ella pictured the tiny oriental climbing up on chairs and tables to reach Ringo's hair, stretching yellow reedlike arms to reach across Ringo's breasts, each the size of a human head. . . One day the little girl wasn't at the beauty shop when Ringo came to have her hair done, and the old Frenchwoman who owned the shop told Ringo the girl had been captured in a raid north of the city. The little girl had been a terrorist. (Loren's laughter started, an ominous chuckling deep in his chest.) "They knew all along she was doing it," Ringo said. "I was the only one who didn't know it. And every other day that sweet little twat did my hair and we would have nice little chats in French, and she would give me a massage, and all the time she probably had a ball of plastic explosive sewed in her panties."

Ringo looked at Loren and they laughed violently, and Edmond laughed, shaking his head from side to side.

Ella glanced at Loren as he laughed, his head tilted back and his mouth open wide, showing his large, white teeth. She looked down at the floor.

Then she felt him staring at her. She turned to her mother. But the old woman sat smiling, her lips moving, whispering, not paying any attention, and it occurred to Ella that that was only natural: why should the old woman need to know what they were talking about? She sat smiling, her head turned to the side, looking out the front window at the orchard.

And still Ella felt Loren staring at her and finally she looked at him. His eyes were steady. They were like black stones. She slowly put her hands in her lap and clasped them tightly together as the trembling began.

"Those women over there are somethin else," Loren said. He was speaking to her. He grinned slowly, his mouth exceedingly wide. "Oriental ginch," he said low. "They may be little, but that don't stop them. That makes it good. That makes it just right."

"Loren is a lover," Ringo said. Ella looked at her. Ringo stared blankly at Loren. There was great stillness in the way Ringo looked at him.

They were all silent, as if waiting. "Sis," Loren said. The word hung in the air like an odor. She turned slowly and looked at him. "Sis, it's funny the way fate is," he said. "You stayed here all your life and me, I got scooted all around. Argentina. Panama. Africa. Cambodia. You name it, I done it. And the funny part is, if I ran into you in a bar in one of those little towns I'd just gone up to you and patted you on the ass and started up the old Lobas line. . ."

"You wouldn't have found your sister in a bar," Ringo said softly, not to him, maybe to Ella. He ignored her.

". . .and you'd gone juicy like *that,*" he snapped his large fingers, making a loud smack, as if he had struck her, and maybe it was a signal, for he got up, staring intently at her, his eyes not blinking, and he came slowly across the room. Extending his hand and crouching silently as he approached, walking on his toes, he said, "and while the *mariachis* rattle their red little hearts," he took her hand and she slowly stood, her face stiff. She stared at the collar of his shirt. She could smell the musk, apple smell of his breath. When she was standing, he drew her against him, put his arm around her waist and held her tight against him, as if he would press her completely into him. He bent down and put his face to hers until their noses touched, her eyes nearly closed but still seeing the black liquid of his eyes, "and we would dance," he whispered, barely moving his thick lips, and he moved her, turned, and they danced, "and we would talk and get friendly," he moved his head from side to side, rubbing his nose against hers.

". . .some music on the radio," Ella heard her mother say from a great distance. She and Loren stood there together, his arm around her waist, heavy, and his unblinking eyes didn't look away from her.

There was music and they started moving again. "Slowly," he whispered. "Slow. Make it last. Make it last," and she breathed hard. He was holding her too tightly, the room was hot, she was weak, she would die, and as she took a deep breath, the air was hot, it was his breath, and she knew he was breathing into her, their lips nearly touching.

He turned his head to the side. "Edmond. Dance with Ringo. She's a great dancer. Great. Just don't let her get in your pants is all. Eh Ringo? Eh?"

She didn't answer, but stood up and went over to Edmond. "Come on," she said.

Loren turned his face back to Ella and put his cheek to hers, his lips touching her ear, and he whispered, "You're nice, Ella. Real nice. I mean it. Ella. I never did think about you all this time. You know? Ella. Huh. Like Cinderella. I guess everybody says that to you, uh? Like a guy I know his name was John Kennedy and everybody wants to shake his hand. But you're nice, Ella. Real nice, and you know what I mean nice? Huh?" She couldn't speak. "I mean you're nice like it'd be a treat to kiss you. You know, slow, easy, just soft and easy. . ." and moving his lips along her cheek to her mouth, he slowly put his lips to hers, lightly, and he moved his lips back and forth until her lips hurt, were open, and he touched her lips with his tongue. Slowly back and forth it traced her lower lip, her upper lip, and her lips came together on his tongue and his tongue slid into her mouth.

And immediately out again before she could make herself think, and he turned his head to the side, then turned away from her, his arm brushing her hips as it moved down from her waist, and he talked to Ringo and Edmond, and Ella blinked and held her breath. Among the old dark furniture, the darkening windows, the walls closing in, she saw her mother sitting beside the radio, smiling, her eyes closed.

Ringo and Edmond stopped dancing and listened as Loren talked to them. Ella didn't hear what he said. Then Edmond was in front of her, talking, his round face intent, and she heard him saying, ". . .then just go ahead and stay if you'd like to. There's no reason I can see for you to come back today when you can just as easy wait till tomorrow. Since it's been so long since you've seen your brother."

Ella blinked at him. Loren took her arm and guided her away from Edmond toward Ringo, and Ringo, her face cold, her eyes large and blank, reached out to her. Ella obediently lifted her hand and let Ringo lead her to the bedroom where Loren and Ringo had slept last night.

Ringo closed the door and sat down on the bed. She took off her high heels and her hose. She stood up and went out of the room. Ella stood before the old, time-bent mirror on the dressing table. She saw Loren in her face: the nose, mouth, and eyes—especially the eyes. All her life this face had been hers and not hers, she had known her face and not known it at all. And now she was knowing. It was coming up slowly, dark and wet, a reflection from a mirror placed far beneath the surface of water. She and Loren were the same flesh. She had believed this was gone, but it wasn't gone. Neither was gone the day when she stood in the door of the barnloft and looked out at the orchard and saw her father come running toward the house, his head and face and his shirt and overalls glistening red. From that day on Loren and most of her life were gone—though she saw, in the crooked mirror, that when he left, she had gone with him and now she was back again, and she was now at last seeing herself.

It happened again, with her looking in the mirror: in the morning of that day Loren dragged her to the barn and that afternoon of the same day she got to her feet and looked out the door of the loft and just then she heard the shouting far away in the orchard. She thought the cows had jumped the fence and were into the orchard again and that Loren and her father were driving them out, and she forgot herself and looked out and in the distance . . . or was it near? She couldn't know what she had seen and what she had deduced, maybe even invented by later thinking about it again and again, through long nights that were so silent now that both men, with their snoring that shook the small house, were gone.

She heard the car start—her and Edmond's car—and she went to the bedroom window and pulled the shade aside. Edmond was in the car, Loren was standing beside it. Stiffly, Edmond raised his hand and waved to her. It seemed he had been waiting for her to look out at him, as if Loren, who in his way knew all things, had told him that Ella would be looking out in a few moments and that he should wave goodbye to her when she did.

She watched as Edmond drove out of the barn lot, and she watched as the car slowly moved onto the gravel road and drove away. Loren walked toward the house.

She took down her dress and stepped out of it.

Ringo came back into the room. She had taken off her make-up. Her face was exceedingly pale, and she held her head down. "Put this on." She handed Ella a silk dress—green, orange, and red.

Ella's hands burned when she touched it.

"It'll fit you. Loren got it for me. He likes it. It hooks at the side. Like a sarong. It fits all sizes."

Ringo turned away and took off her dress. Her body was immense and white. She put on a full-length tight black dress with long sleeves. She stood at the mirror and took off the large, elaborate blond wig. Beneath it her hair was black and slick. She put the wig in a box and shoved it under the bed. From under the bed she took another, smaller box. It contained a black turban which she put on her head.

When she was finished she turned from the mirror. "Get dressed." She crossed the room to Ella and took the silk dress from her hand.

She stepped behind Ella and unsnapped her brassiere. Ella tried to hold it up to her breasts, but Ringo jerked the straps off her shoulders and pulled it away. She stepped in front of her and though Ella held her head down, she could tell Ringo was looking at her breasts, first one, then the other. Then she looked down at Ella's slip. "Take that off. Everything. With this dress you wear nothing," and she watched while Ella obeyed.

Naked, still standing with her head down, Ella stared at the floor, then at her breasts, waiting for Ringo to speak. But she said nothing and Ella looked at Ringo's feet, at the sharp-toed black shoes beneath the long black dress, and slowly she raised her head, looking up the length of Ringo, and when she was to Ringo's face she forgot herself, her nakedness.

Ringo's face was stone gray, and it was as gaunt and drawn as the face of the old woman in the other room who sat by the radio with her eyes closed, dreaming of her son, while her son sat, panting, across the room from her.

The three of them went to town to Zeppels, then to Troy's Bar, and then they drove ten miles to the next town, stopped at roadhouses along the way, and then they went to all the bars in the next town.

Ringo drove the car and Ella and Loren rode in the back. She stared out the window at the night. He pulled her toward him and she lay against him. He unhooked the dress and opened it and lay his hand on her breast over her heart. Her breath raised and lowered her breast under his hand. The night slid by the window.

At another town, at another bar, they danced and when they didn't dance they sat side by side in a booth and he talked to her. He talked to her constantly, and his hand was on her under the table. Across the table Ringo sat.

They left and went out to the car and when she got into the back seat she reached out to him and again he unhooked her dress and she writhed and scooted in the seat until she was out of the dress. Ringo drove the car down a perfectly straight road, on and on, and they met no cars, they passed no towns, farm houses, there was complete darkness beyond the pavement grayed by the headlights of their car, and the car was then descending through the night. It was going straight down.

Then she believed she saw flickers of light in the black. She blinked her eyes, waited.

She saw it again, as if something was running alongside the car—perhaps a great gray dog, or a gray horse, or a man dissolving.

She sat up, her face to the window, and the flickering was more distinct.

They were driving down the orchard road. It was the back road that come up from the river and passed through the orchard.

They were going incredibly fast. But the orchard road was bumpy, an old road unused except, years ago, during the harvest of the apples. But the car moved smoothly.

She looked up and saw the gray trees, row on row, blurring by the window, and she fell back slowly as she realized the car wasn't on the orchard road, but that they were in the orchard itself, they were sliding down the long, long row straight toward the barn and she rose and looked over the black shoulder of Ringo. Ahead, in the distance, somehow visible, but dimly, beyond the cold swath of light from the headlights, framed in the point of the narrowing V of gray trees, she saw the house and the barn, and in the barn, though it was still a great distance away, she saw the loft door was open and she closed her eyes just as she began to see the small write outline of a girl crouching in the loft door, looking out.

The car stopped. She lay with her eyes closed. She listened and heard nothing. Then Ringo spoke low, in a strange language, not a language but a whine, rising and falling. Then she got out of the car and quietly shut the door.

Ella turned and tried to see Loren's face.

"Let's go," he said and lifted her until she was standing outside the car and she saw their mother's house hovering in the darkness.

She followed him into the house. He left the room dark and turning to her, pushed the dress off her shoulders. She stood with her arms to her sides, waiting.

"Father was buried on the hill back of the orchard," she heard herself saying. She closed her eyes. "Do you remember the orchard the way it used to be? One time you and I were in a tree, all the trees running out from it in long lines. We were in the top and everything was silent and nothing was moving. It was like nothing had ever happened and nothing was ever going to happen. Everything was gone, and we were even different people. We weren't even people.

"When father was killed you left and never came back."

He pulled her down to the floor.

"I wrote you letters and gave them to Mother and I guess she read them first before she put them away, or threw them away, I don't know, but then I guess she stopped reading them. Maybe I ought to ask her if she kept them. It would be interesting to. . . But they would be sad. Maybe even you would think they were sad if you read them. They were like love letters. And I knew they were love letters. That ought to please you. But maybe I wrote them as much to Father as to you, even if I put your name on them and it was you I was talking to." He began kissing her neck, her breasts.

"I couldn't sleep for a long time. Mother couldn't either. We got up again and again, every night. Mother would tell me I should go to sleep and I said I would and then we'd go back and lay awake in bed. Always I could hear the wind blowing in the orchard.

"Sometimes I still have a nightmare and I see a man running down in the orchard. I call Mother to the back door and when she gets there the man turns off the row he was running down and he runs through the trees and we look down the rows and he is running toward the house, he is coming toward us. . .

"And I know . . . at the back of my mind I know it's . . . the man who killed Father, but I don't say it to Mother. But the minute I see him running toward the house I know it's the man who killed him. . .

"Loren, where were you? Why didn't you help Father? Where were you?"

He answered by slowly spreading her legs.

"Do you think of death as you travel in the same skin with it, even in sleep, an animal with lives like unending memories? Or does being death take it back to meaning nothing?" He lowered his head. He pierced her with his tongue. She stopped.

She opened her eyes to the dark room. The ceiling was streaked with gray lines. Without words, with nothing, she felt what he was doing and she heard herself moaning and she stopped herself. She just lay there, listening to the sounds he was making. Finally he stopped.

Apart from her, somewhere in the darkness, he seemed to hide.

Then she saw him in the gray light emerging naked from the darkness as if he were stepping out of a black door, and he came slowly toward her, his hands at his sides, and he was swollen enormous, a fist on a forearm.

Ella was at the stove pouring another cup of coffee when Ringo came out of the bedroom. She said good morning to Ella's mother, glanced at Ella, and sat down at the table.

Ella's mother went on talking about when she and Ella's father came to this part of the country. They had two different families of children before Ella and Loren were born, and those two bunches of children had gone away, she didn't know where all they had gone, and most of them were old by now, had grandchildren of their own. The old woman laughed and said it seemed that those other children of hers were older than she was, much older.

Ella left the stove and sat at the table across from Ringo. Ringo looked at her and said, "Did you have fun last night?" Her face was again large, bright and smooth, but puffed by the layers of make-up.

Ella looked away. Her mother was now talking about all the children who had died. There had been at least two, three bunches of children who had died over the years.

"He'll stay in bed all day," Ringo said, her voice below the steady drone of the old woman's voice. "He's not sleeping. But he'll stay in there. But don't try to go in to him. He wouldn't like that. And later on, maybe this afternoon, he'll call me and I'll go in to him. You see how it is?"

Ella stared at her. The gray irises of Ringo's eyes had tiny cracks of black. They were like cinders. She had seen everything. She had traveled with Loren and she had seen everything he did. She loved it, and she would stay with him until, eventually, he killed her.

"Are you bleeding?" she whispered.

Ella didn't answer. She looked away, then said, "Yes."

Ringo nodded, pleased, and lit a cigarette. She leaned back, folding her arms under her breasts. The long cigarette drooped in a corner of her mouth, and the eye above it squinted against the slow line of smoke moving across her face. "He killed a girl once," she said.

Ella's mother went on, chantlike.

"A Korean girl. He paid twenty dollars for her. We were in Pusan doing salvage. He paid her family twenty dollars for her and took her into the warehouse. He killed her." She smiled slowly. "I guess you know how. You know. . ." Her tone changed. She spoke without the flat hardness of before. Now it was too far the opposite, chatty, and as she talked, the cigarette in her mouth wobbled, bobbed up and down, and spilled ashes. "You know it's really amazing. I've never seen another one like it. Anywhere. Have you?" Ella didn't answer. "The first time I saw it . . . I remember. I didn't think it was real. It's amazing." She paused, staring at Ella. "And you're his sister." She laughed.

Then her tone changed again. Her eyes dimmed. The cigarette had burned down almost to her lips. "That don't matter to him. He likes it all." She took the cigarette from her lips and looked at it, then ground it out in the saucer of Ella's cup. "Why did he kill his old man?" she said.

The room roared with coldness. The silence was like glass around the three of them, and Ella knew her mother had been listening and knew—had been listening all along and knew everything—and the glass of silence was broken when Ella and her mother spoke at the same time, the old woman chanting loudly, or moaning in her old-woman, animal way, and Ella heard herself saying, "He didn't kill Father. That isn't what happened. It's wrong."

But Ringo wasn't listening. She had lit another cigarette and now sat with her eyes squinted closed, and Ella knew she was gone back to all those places where terrible things happened and she was trying to undo, in the way of a woman (in that part of her that was still a woman) all those things, trying to make them better by recreating them from their memories—just as he recreated them, but not merely in reverie but in his violent action, each time again making the same error, each time at the fatal moment plunging over into that loose dark air where everything happens.

Ella was talking, saying what for years she had dreamed, saying she looked out the loft door and saw her father and he was bleeding, he was torn, he had been chopped, and the man chasing him with a hatchet in each hand was *not* Loren, that the man had been too far away for her to see, and there hadn't been a man there at all, her father had fallen under the harrow. Her mother was looking at her through the room buzzing with words like flies. Her mother's eyes were sharp, clear.

The afternoon was as bright, as yellow as fire, as if she and her mother had just now come back into the kitchen from the field, sweating, and his blood soaked through their dresses, her mother's face wet with sweat but calm.

They were silent, the old woman choked on her prayers, Ringo gone, in Panama, Brazil, Korea, Vietnam. Ella sat there, still feeling him, and for a long time the only sound was the wind, far away, in the orchard.

Then the old woman was looking out at the orchard again, and she started talking, on and on, about the families she had given birth to, and from the other room they heard him.

He called low, not uttering the name but growling. Ringo got up and walked slowly to the bedroom door, waited, then entered.

Ella listened, and then the noise began. The old woman, oblivious in time, talked, and though she talked, perhaps she heard the sounds from the bedroom. Perhaps she felt the rattling vibrations that shook the house, and perhaps she heard beneath her droning their strong, urgent voices like the snarling voices of wolves.

When the house stopped shaking there was a long silence.

The old woman slept in her chair by the window, her head hanging.

And later, after the long day, Ella heard the car coming down the road. She calmly went out of the house.

Edmond waved to her and got out of the car. He was talking excitedly about what had happened—Walter's truck had broken down at Richmond, and Edmond and Lloyd had to go down and unload it and get another truck, and Carl Johnson had called in the afternoon and said he would lease Edmond the lot next to the store but Edmond would have to do the building himself, and Edmond was going to have Ella talk to the Smith girls again about their father and his loan. . .

At first what he said came from far off. But Ella began slowly recognizing the names and then suddenly she knew what he was saying. She answered him.

With the first words she spoke she saw him listening intently, listening with deep satisfaction that this part of him was back.

VICTIMS

Mr. Conroy was gathering his papers when his secretary ran into his office. "The President. Someone shot him. In Dallas."

"You're sure of this."

She nodded, big-eyed.

"Very well," Mr. Conroy said. He put the papers in a folder and closed it.

She stood in front of his desk. "What should I do?"

"What do you mean?"

"I just thought . . . " She lifted her hands. "The conference with Durkin and La Brosse. Should I cancel it?"

"Why?"

"Oh." She backed away, then turned and went out.

Five minutes later Durkin and La Brosse's office called and canceled the conference.

Mr. Conroy flicked off the intercom. "It happens again," he said softly. He rose from his desk and started for the door—and the room started spinning. He made it to a chair and leaned back, breathing through his mouth. *It happens again.* On wheels, all things roll swiftly away and the sky opens like a hangar roof . . . and above—nothing. He clenched his eyes and made himself breathe evenly. He tried not to think. *It happens again,* and he could not stop it. "My boy," he whispered. "My poor boy." He exhaled all the air from his lungs and locked his arms around his chest. But his lungs pulled air into themselves, and the world was full of people.

His face was sweating. He wiped it with his handkerchief.

At Mr. Conroy's club the saloon was crowded and noisy, and the barman was playing Sousa over the P.A. system. Someone shouted his name and he saw Peters, Hogan, and Brookman at the bar. He joined them. Everyone was drunk with excitement. Then word came that Kennedy was dead. A loud cheer went up.

Red-faced, breathing hard, Mr. Conroy toasted the future with them. His glass clinked so hard with Brookman's their glasses broke. Brookman roared with laughter.

Downstairs, Chuck was alone. "Hello, Mr. Conroy. Did you hear about . . . ?"

"Let's have a game. I'll be out in a minute." He had his coat and tie off and was into the locker room before Chuck could reply.

Mr. Conroy won the first game, slamming the ball against the gray wall. "Your serve," Mr. Conroy said, sweat glistening on his face, and tossed the ball to Chuck.

"My heart's not in it," Chuch said.

"Serve."

Mr. Conroy was winning again when Chuck took off his gloves. "I can't. I'm sorry, Mr. Conroy. You can report me if you want to. But I just can't."

Mr. Conroy watched him keenly as Chuck turned to the wall. He was crying. Mr. Conroy left the court without speaking.

The steam room was shut down. He looked in the massage room, but Hans wasn't there.

Mr. Conroy took a quick shower, dressed, and returned to the saloon. The celebration had ended except for the band music and the same dozen or so who were in the bar every afternoon.

He walked briskly back to his office building and went down to the garage. The attendant brought his car. Mr. Conroy squealed the tires as he took off, then blared his horn and skidded out the exit, the front bumper slicing over the sidewalk—"At the knees," he said out loud, and remembered Brookman's warning several weeks ago when Mr. Conroy gave him a lift home: "Keep it up and you'll kill someone. Take up hunting, Conroy. It honest to God helps. You know what I mean?" Mr. Conroy knew exactly what Brookman meant. Once a year Brookman went to Alaska—and hunting got rid of it for him. And everyone hunts, Brookman went on—the only question is *what* you hunt.

Mr. Conroy went to the Vendome Hotel. A waitress was setting tables in the empty dining room. "Where's Kitty?" Mr. Conroy asked her.

"In the kitchen. I'll get her."

"Don't bother." He went through the dining room to the swinging door to the kitchen. He called, "Kitty!" before he was through the door and then saw her, wearing a long black dress, her blond hair swirled intricately. She was smoking a cigarette and talking to two waitresses.

She came toward him, "Well, Mr. Conroy. How are . . . ?"

"Let's go upstairs."

She blinked. Her smile hardened but didn't leave her face. "Not so loud, okay?"

"Come on."

"I can't. The dining room opens in twenty minutes."

"Tell them your mother's sick. Or you can't work because of Kennedy."

"You've heard about it. Isn't it just awful? We heard it was some Cubans who came up from . . . "

He took her arm. "Come on."

"Let go," she said. "All right. I'll be up in a few minutes. Go on up. I'll have to think of something to tell Louie."

"Tell him about Kennedy."

"He already knows."

"I meant tell him you don't feel like working because of Kennedy."

"Are you okay?"

"Yes."

"You look . . . peculiar."

He smiled faintly, not looking at her.

"I mean strange. It's almost like you're someone else."

Then she patted his arm. “Go on up. Five minutes. Can you wait that long?” She smiled a wide, sly smile.

When he left Kitty and the hotel, Mr. Conroy drove across town and parked in the alley behind a large Victorian house. George was smoking on the back porch—Russell didn’t allow his cigars inside. “How do, Mr. Conroy,” George said. “You hear they shot the President in the head?”

“Who’s here?” he asked as he went up the steps.

“They all here ‘cept Lo. He outa town on business.”

George unlocked the back door and followed Mr. Conroy down the gray, sour hallway to the stairs. On the second floor, where the lights burned inside the sealed, blacked-out windows, Russell sat on his throne. “Mr. Conroy!” he called and got up with effort. “So good to see you again. I guess you heard they . . . ”

“Jimmy,” Mr. Conroy said.

"Jimmy?" he said. "Skinny Jimmy?"

George left the room. Russell chatted and offered Mr. Conroy a drink, candy, a cigarette . . . George returned and nodded. Mr. Conroy followed him through the curtained doorway and down the hall.

His wife Martha had already eaten and was out for bridge, the maid told him.

Mr. Conroy changed clothes and went to his studio on the third floor. He put a fresh canvas on the easel. Now and then he heard himself—his voice echoing in the high-ceilinged room. Martha called his name several times before he turned and stared at her.

She wore silver fox over a black dress. “I suppose you heard about Kennedy,” she said. “Everyone is talking about it. I’m already tired of it and it just happened today. What’s that supposed to be?”

He turned to it. Clots of paint slowly bled down the canvas. When he looked away again the door was closed.

The bars closed, only a few stragglers were on the street—some drunks on a corner, two men and a woman, each looking off in a different direction. Mr. Conroy stopped the car beside them. The woman looked at him, then away, aimlessly—she hadn't seen him. One of the men tilted his head back and started yelling at the sky.

In the next block a man was piled on himself as if he had been hammered into the sidewalk. Mr. Conroy pulled to the curb and hauled him into the back seat.

He drove to the edge of the city and came to a wide plain covered with junk. Mr. Conroy followed a dirt road, then stopped and cut the headlights. He listened to the heavy breathing from the back seat.

Mr. Conroy switched on the dome light and looked over his shoulder. The face was flat under the light. The man groaned and without opening his eyes said loudly "Are we on our way?" Mr. Conroy got out and slammed the door. The smoke of burning rubber hung in the air.

He drove all night, following the freeway to its first junction and turning onto that highway, and turning onto a different highway at every junction. But at the first gray of dawn he was driving down the empty streets of the city.

He stopped and pulled the man out, groaning and mumbling, and leaned him against a wall. Mr. Conroy waited again, standing over him. He turned and got in the car.

"What are you doing in here?" Martha looked at the clock. "It's six o'clock. What's the matter with you?" She pulled up the sheet over her nightgown. Her short gray hair, usually covered with a wig, sprigged up in tufts.

"They killed Kennedy," Mr. Conroy said.

"I know. Now leave me alone."

"Talk to me, goddamnit."

She stared at him. "All right. Fine. But it's six o'clock in the morning."

"They shot him in the head."

"Yes. So?"

He touched her head. "Feel that."

"I feel it."

His hand dropped and he looked away. "What can we do?" he whispered.

"I don't know what you mean. There's nothing to do."

"Move over," he said.

"No."

"I only want to lie down."

"Lie down in your own room."

"I can't. Please."

"Just to lie down. Nothing else."

She moved over and he lay on top the covers.

"I want to adopt a kid," Mr. Conroy said.

"That is ridiculous. I never heard anything so ridiculous in all my life."

For a long time he stared at the ceiling. Then he said, "Yes," and closed his eyes. Mr. Conroy dreamed about his office. He was working, talking to people, and no one mentioned Kennedy. When Mr. Conroy woke, Martha was gone.

He sat up and saw the maid standing in the door. "What?"

"It's eight-thirty, Mr. Conroy."

"All right." She left the room. His body ached, and he believed he had a fever—"Good," he said. It would get him through the day.

IN THE MOOD OF ZEBRAS

I looked out the window and fifty or sixty people were milling in the front yard. I didn't like the looks of it, even though they had brought their children along. I ran out the back door and sneaked around the side of the house. Without their noticing, I slipped in among them and listened, trying to find out what they were up to, but they were mumbling. Then one of them recognized me and shouted out, "Why, Boots Ladd is standing right here. Where'd you come from?"

"I was inside the house. I came out."

"Oh. Out the back door?"

I nodded.

They formed a big circle and sat down on the grass. Some kids ran squealing through the center until their mothers caught them and made them sit. There followed a long silence.

"Boots," Walter Skates said, taking it on himself to be spokesman since no one else would, "we're all of us sort of perturbed."

"What's the matter?" I asked as if I didn't know.

"Well, it's not really any of our concern . . . "

"Yes, it is," someone pitched in and others agreed. A mumble passed around the circle.

"Well, we *do* live here. And our families have lived here for generations and generations, for years and years," Walter said. "So it is our business, in that way."

"It's them mules," a woman said from the outer edge of the circle.

They waited. I looked around at them, then up at the sky. It was purple in a sunset that turned the fields blue and made sounds and movement hover in the still air.

"Well," I said slowly. "Them mules . . . "

Then distantly we heard my uncle down in the creek meadow, yipping and yowing as he ran with the animals. Likely, it had been that commotion that caused suspicion. People naturally wonder when an old man starts spending the better part of his time out in a meadow with mules.

As I was thinking this, everyone sitting in the circle turned and some moved to clear a way. My uncle came up the hill, and one of the animals was walking along with him as mannerly as could be.

"Evenin', Boots," my uncle said.

"Let's get to the point," Walter Skates said as the circle closed behind my uncle and the animal. "We want to know just what you're up to."

"Yes. What are those things you're keeping down there in that meadow?"

"Mules," I said. "Six, counting this one."

The animal turned and looked at me. He rolled his big eyes with very much expression—which you'd seldom, if ever, see a mule do—and while it looked at me, its jaw quivered and its lips drew back in what was most certainly a smile.

"No one has ever seen a mule like that. Look at that thing." They were right, of course. My uncle and I had painted the animals gray to fool people.

"And the size on it. Why, that's no way near the shape of a mule."

They all stared at me.

I shrugged.

"See," one of them said. "I told you Boots wouldn't admit anything."

They were gone, my uncle too. I led the animal down to the creek meadow, and it trotted on ahead.

The meadow is bordered on the outside by a cliff that scares the little creek, keeps it from spilling itself over the edge. It is hardly what most people would consider a creek, apart from its creek cowardice about becoming a waterfall. At its widest a man can easily step across it. But it never dries up, and like a true creek, no one knows where it starts or where it ends—at least no one in our county. At the edge of the meadow, which is also the county line, the cliff falls hundreds, perhaps thousands of feet—no one know just how far because no one has measured it. Such a task would take the measuring party into the next county and few if any of us would be willing to go, even to measure our cliff (which the next county probably consider *their* cliff). Our county is a table, breaking at the cliff; the next county, far below, is another table. I have heard that beyond that county there is a still lower table.

Dusk was ending. Purple, blue, and black lay in the meadow beneath the stars already bright in the summer sky.

My uncle sprawled in the middle of the meadow with the animals around him, their heads turned toward him, as if listening to him. My uncle spent most of his days and late into each night out here. When he would finally come up to the house, he seldom slept but sat in his rocking chair by the window, looking down toward the meadow, and at dawn, without touching his head to his pillow, he would slip out the front door and I would see him walking down the meadow, leaving a path in the wet grass.

"Hello," I called. The animals looked my way, then back to my uncle.

"We should go before it's too late," he said low, not to me. I sat crosslegged a ways from him. One of the animals leaned over and politely sniffed me, then drew its head back on its long, powerful neck.

"India," my uncle said sadly. He was talking to me. "It's a million miles away and after you get there they won't let you in. And China's the same. But they let you in if you got a good reason, and these things of ours will get us in anywhere." That was what he had called them from the beginning—our things. "And I'm not talking about stupid circus sideshows and such as that." Which he *had* talked about at first. "I mean, just go up and say, 'Looky here. We've got these six marvelous things.' And everybody will stop and look at them and . . . "

He went on but I barely listened, leaning back against one of the animals. Always before, my uncle had been satisfied leaving things as they were. But nothing had ever come along and asked him whether he wanted to stay here or traipse off to the world looking for people.

The animals turned their heads toward the cliff, their ears pricked.

I had never said a word to him about the way he was carrying on. Whatever I said would have sounded like what the people from town had asked *me.* And I knew my uncle could answer me no better than I answered them.

Then my uncle stopped talking and jumped up without startling the animals. He ran up the meadow toward the barn.

I lay back again, feeling the great heart pounding inside the animal I was leaning against. The sky shone with more stars than I had ever seen. Light rippled across the sky in slow, steady pulses.

Again the animals turned toward the cliff, and I looked too. But of course no one or no thing could come from that direction, not even the noise of people far away.

My uncle came down the meadow singing, and as if it were singing along with him, there was the squeaking of the bail of a rusty bucket that had hung in our barn for years.

My uncle stood in the glare of starlight, the rusty bucket in his hand, and announced he was leaving. The animals silently got to their feet.

My uncle asked if I wanted to go too. I didn't know what to say. My uncle and the animals stared at me. "Yes and no," I mumbled.

My uncle told me to help him get them ready, even if I wasn't going, and he tossed me a large cloth. He dipped the bucket into the creek and we commenced to wash off the camouflage we had painted on the animals when we found them grazing in our front yard that morning two weeks earlier, one of them standing with its forefeet on the porch steps.

The animals cooperated as we washed them. After we sloshed them down they backed away a safe distance, reared up, and shook themselves, the spray sparkling in the starlight. In a few minutes the gray paint was washed off, even from their hooves and they pranced, their dazzling black and white stripes shining under the sea of starlight, and they were impatient, they couldn't stand still, they nudged us, bumped against us, almost knocking us down.

"Come on," my uncle shouted to me as he leaped onto the back of one of them.

I couldn't move.

"Come on."

I stood staring. "I want to, but . . . "

And there was a sound that this time even I heard at the same instant the zebras and my uncle turned, and we all stared toward the cliff and the sea of sky beyond it.

Maybe I tried explaining. I can't remember. Maybe the explanations that now come to mind are justifications I have needed over the years.

But while I was talking, the zebras slowly turned, their black and white stripes starting a dizzying ripple, and I was running with them, still trying to talk, shouting at first, though their heads were lifted as if I were already far behind, and my uncle was no longer listening, in fact I could no longer even see him as I ran as fast as I could down the meadow, and then the shaking of the earth under their hooves stopped, though they were still running, and the only sound was my own loud breathing and my heart.

As though running into a wall, at the cliff I was stopped. Another step and I would have paced off into the sky. The zebras soared off and in seconds were gone—the last sign of them not the sight of them flying through the air, but the sound of a tight squeak, as if all the zebras and my uncle too had squeezed through a point of light in the sky.

FICTION COLLECTIVE

Books in Print

The Second Story Man by Mimi Albert
Searching for Survivors by Russell Banks
Reruns by Jonathan Baumbach
Things in Place by Jerry Bumpus
Museum by B. H. Friedman
Reflex and Bone Structure by Clarence Major
The Secret Table by Mark Mirsky
The Comatose Kids by Seymour Simckes
Twiddledum Twaddledum by Peter Spielberg
98.6 by Ronald Sukenick
Statements: New Fiction, edited by Fiction Collective authors